T0167731

THE WHALE HOUSE

AND OTHER STORIES

ACKNOWLEDGEMENTS

To get a book out of your head and into the hands of readers would not be possible without the help of so many people. This book could not have existed without the early attention of the late Wayne Brown. I am also indebted to my Lesley University mentors Hester Kaplan, Michael Lowenthal and Tony Eprile who helped me articulate these stories on the page and did a lot of hand holding. To Keith Jardim who read early drafts of this manuscript; to the Bocas Dream Team of Marina, Nicholas, and Anna for putting Caribbean literature on the front burner; to Ivan Charles for teaching me the joys of spelunking; to Courtenay Williams for invaluable details on white Holden Belmont cars with tinted windows and the people who drove them in the early 1970s; to Frances, Tara, and Jeannine for too many things to mention and finally to Jeremy and Hannah at Peepal Tree who took a chance on me. Thank you.

To my mother and grandmother who taught me the ways of women, my father who taught me responsibility and how to take care, and my ever supportive sister, Jennifer. There are not enough words.

SHARON MILLAR

THE WHALE HOUSE

AND

OTHER STORIES

PEEPAL TREE

First published in Great Britain in 2015
Peepal Tree Press Ltd
17 King's Avenue
Leeds LS6 1QS
England

© 2015 Sharon Millar

ISBN13: 9781845232498

All rights reserved
No part of this publication may be
reproduced or transmitted in any form
without permission

This is a work of fiction. All the characters
appearing in the stories are fictitious.
Any resemblance to real persons,
living or dead, is purely coincidental

Supported using public funding by
ARTS COUNCIL
ENGLAND

CONTENTS

To Ross and Hayley

Carmelita

Weeks before Christmas, in the hills of the Northern range, a boy disappears from home. He is seventeen years old. His mother, Carmelita Nunes, calls on the Orisha gods and prays to St. Anthony, the patron saint of lost things. Her son is not yet a man and she knows that makes him both more dangerous and more vulnerable. On the first day of his absence, she draws a thick black line through the almanac hanging on the kitchen wall. On the third day, a black Friday, she dresses in her best clothes and calls a taxi. When she passes through the village, sitting in the back seat, some people raise their hands in gentle waves while others stare, their arms still. The village had lost hunting dogs and caged parrots, but never a boy. Even the ageing white French Creole, who has never spoken to her, and old man Lum Fatt, who still dreams of China, come to see her drive down the winding road towards the police station.

Carmelita was not naïve, but weeks before when her two other children had come to the house to talk about Daniel she'd turned her head and raised the volume on the radio. First Oriana had come and then Johnny. It was only after Daniel had raised his hand to her, the hand moving from his side with lightning violence, that there was talk of sending him to Johnny in town. Send him, Oriana had said, send him so that Johnny could teach him about respect. He'd stayed with Johnny and his wife for less than two days. Oh God, Carmelita thought, after Johnny called to say Daniel was heading home.

"You can't talk some sense into him?" Her voice echoed down the telephone wire.

"I have Lilla to think of, Ma. She's afraid of him."

Most of the young boys make their money growing weed in the forest, ducking and hiding from the police helicopters that swooped like clumsy dragonflies before chop-chopping their way back to the city. That's all it was, she thought, nothing the other boys aren't doing.

To keep him at home, Carmelita showed him how to curry birds: chickens, ducks, pigeons. Cutting, chopping, frying, stewing. She held a plucked duck over the open fire, singeing the skin; cut the fat gland off the end of a chicken, and killed a pigeon quietly without breaking its tiny bones. She showed him how to add pimento pepper and ground ginger as her mother had taught her.

"South boys work in oil and town boys work in banks," said Daniel as he watched her cook, "but what happen to the village boys from the north?" He spoke to the duck, sitting cold and pimple-skinned on the counter, not to her.

"You think any tomato or christophene could ever compete with that black gold. Those south boys born into that. It come like they own that fountain of oil. And town boys only eating sushi and managing money market."

The duck was now in the pot, its skin sizzling and browning, mixing with the seasoning, flooding the kitchen with such a good scent that it was as if he were saying something that she wanted to hear, something happy. When she looked up from the pot, his topaz eyes were on her, baleful and sly. She tamped down the doubt that she'd grown this child. Looking away, he shook his head, a quick movement, like a dog trying to get water out of his ear.

Later, he told her that sometimes they worked from a small base on Chachachacare, the abandoned island that once housed nuns and lepers – he'd seen women, dark silhouettes on the pirogues. They'll kill me if they know I talk, he told her later that night. They tell me so all the time.

"Who is 'they', Daniel?" she asked. "Who is 'they'?

But he was too busy eating his duck to answer her.

That night she looked up the word sushi in the dictionary, but it was not listed in her old pocket version. But she did find the word cocaine.

It is only after they pass the large immortelle tree, the big taxi juddering into first gear on the hairpin turn, that Carmelita allows herself to breathe. Now she is out of view, she can stop feeling shame. No doubt the villagers will have milled around in the road after she left, looking for the silvery flashes of the big Chevrolet as it rounded the corners of the hill.

Mr. Ali is only called up to the village in emergencies. Right next to her on the backseat is the faint brown stain from when Myrtle nearly sliced off her finger and Carmelita had to hold her hand up over her head while Mr. Ali barrelled down the hill. Myrtle is a good friend, thirty years of looking at each other across a hedge, day and night, and minding each other's children made them like family. Myrtle had come over last night to tell her the village talk.

"People saying that Dan cross Chale Jamiah," she said. "Is one of two things happen to him, Carmelita. Either Jamiah's people pick him up or the police hold him. The only thing we could do is pray."

Carmelita had run this conversation over and over in her mind all night. She'd played it like a movie, each word an image. Everyone knew Chale Jamiah grew tomatoes. No one dared to say that tomatoes couldn't build that big house in town; there was even talk that he'd bought an oil rig. You could sell tomatoes from morning to night but even the simplest child could do the math. Tomatoes didn't buy oil rigs. He was a big whistler as well. They said he could whistle any tune. A nice looking man who whistled and grew tomatoes, she'd met Jamiah once years ago when he'd come to the house to pay his respects after Frank had died. Farmer to farmer, he'd said, and she hadn't thought any more of it.

When Frank collapsed in the lettuce bed at the side of the house, Carmelita was soaping baby Daniel's head, shielding his golden eyes, he chittering in the lukewarm water of his kitchen sink bath, little happy chirrups of contentment as the water poured over his head. She'd run to go to Frank leaving Daniel in the water, wailing and slippery. By the time Mr. Ali made it up the hill, Myrtle had covered Frank's face with a flowered sheet. After this Carmelita began to pray, imagining her prayers carrying the soul of her husband. She'd picked roses for Mother Mary while keeping her eyes open for five-toed hens to woo the Orisha gods. On some nights she'd burned incense for Ganesh who shared a shrine with Jesus under the hog plum tree. She wasn't taking chances with Frank's soul.

In the town below, Mr. Ali let her out into a river of heated bodies – people swimming like guabines on the pavements. On the main boulevard, Guyanese and various small island immigrants hock their wares. Cheap panties and pirated DVDs, strung side by side on collapsible display racks, hover above dirty drain water. At the police station, she looks for Corporal Beaubrun, a distant cousin.

He's in the middle of breakfast, smoked herring and bake on his desk. Wiping his hands on the seat of his pants, he comes towards her. He's a good-looking boy. Tall and dark with a square head and a nose carved like an answer to his heavy brow. At the counter he takes his time pulling his pen out of his pocket.

"I hear you having some trouble with your last one," he says.

"He misses a father's hand."

"How long has he been gone?"

"Since Wednesday morning. He said he was coming down here to do some business."

"He wasn't in school?"

She shakes her head.

"He has a woman?"

"No." Oh God is this man so dense that he does not understand what she is asking of him. "It might be too late when you all finally decide to look for him," she says carefully.

"You know something you not telling me?"

"No, just worried."

He shuffles a few papers on his desk.

"How long we know each other?" he asks.

"Since primary school, you know that. What's that got to do with this?"

"Sit tight and he will come home. The more trouble you make…"

"To look for a missing child is to make trouble?"

He places the cap back on his pen and glances at his breakfast.

"Come," he says. "Come and talk outside. I'll walk you

out." They leave the station, his hand lightly on her elbow.

"Has he ever told you who he works for?"

He tells her the boys are recruited from villages all over the island. They are well paid to do what they consider easy work. These rural boys know the terrain, the trails through the hills and are handy with their homemade pipe-guns. They are routinely moved around the island to fill gaps in an army of small-time criminals. If Daniel was ambitious and bright, could he be involved in this?

Carmelita hesitates before answering. What can she say without implicating her son in wrongdoing? Can she believe her youngest son knows right from wrong? Has she been too indulgent with him? She shrugs her shoulders,

"Maybe. I can't say for sure."

Beaubrun sighs and pulls a handkerchief out of his back pocket to wipe his brow.

"I'll call you if I hear anything. I'll make some enquiries."

All day she walks. She passes the old cathedral, cavernous and violet, which stands next to De Freitas Dry Goods with its bags of coffee, cocoa and nutmeg, pigtail buckets, and piles of blue soap. At the end of the street, Chan's Laundry puffs little blasts of starchy steam onto the pavement. In this part of town, blue-bitch stone faces the fronts of the buildings, the corners laid with old ship's ballast. Her father laid blue-bitch all his life – that hard beautiful stone pulled from the earth below the village – a solid, honest life, he always told his children. Work from the land.

She has a picture of Daniel in her hand, holding it up towards the faces of strangers who sidestep her. When the sun begins throwing long shadows, Carmelita veers off the main street, crossing the river that leads to the other side of town. On this side, drinking men spill out from shanty bars with their nasty, stale urine and rum-sweat smells.

Alleys dribble off the main road, wildness taking over. Behind the derelict government housing, the grid-order of the town disappears into indeterminate ends, twisted mazes of collapsing galvanize sheets and open latrines. Here and there golden marigolds grow in discarded truck tires. Further on are the monstrous yards of the scrap iron vendors, rumoured to be the front offices of bustling rent-a-gun operations. Surely someone here must know him. Recognize his face. Tell her something that the police could not.

Down an alley, in the dim light between the buildings, two women sit on an overturned Coca Cola case with a makeshift table between them. One, a coarse-skinned Indian woman is picking out seeds and leaves from a pile of weed, separating it into neat heaps. The second one looks up as Carmelita approaches, her hand motionless over the line of weed on the cigarillo paper. Both women shift at the same time, perfectly synchronised, blocking her view of the table.

"How do you do business?" she whispers. Is it like chicken, she wonders, that you buy by the pound?

The older woman holds up a finger to Carmelita. Wait, she is clearly saying. Don't come any closer. She rises heavily, wearily, rubbing her back as she comes towards Carmelita.

"Do you know him?" Carmelita shows her the picture.

"How much you want?"

"Ahhm, one."

"Just give me a twenty."

The woman takes the photograph from Carmelita.

"Why you looking for this boy?"

"I'm his mother. He's missing."

"Everybody down here know Daniel." The woman makes the sign of the cross before bagging the joint.

"When last you saw him?"

Before the end of the street, she's thrown the joint into a clump of bushes.

When the sun cools she walks home. She stays off the pitch, still radiating the day's heat, walking in the grass at the side of the road, her breath loud in her ears as she climbs and climbs up to her village. Halfway up, her feet stinging from the tiny pebbles on the road, she stops. The plateau overlooks the Gulf of Paria, a big, broody expanse of water. People say that this was where the cocaine crosses, coming from Venezuela. Across the bay, South America is just visible in the dying light. The scarlet ibis are flying home. They fly across the indigo water heading inland towards the swamp. Years before she'd taken Daniel to see the pink birds roost. The birds had landed in rosy blurs, whole ibis families staining the mangroves red.

"Mama, how do they know to come here every night?" he'd asked.

They come, she'd told him, because this is where they sleep. Even the littlest bird knows he must come home to his mama.

When she'd caught her breath, she began walking again.

"Don't cry," says Myrtle, the next morning when she brings Carmelita the newspapers and a ball of cocoa. "Daniel too beautiful to die. He'll be alright. Don't cry, Carmelita."

A lagniappe child, the villagers said when her stomach began to rise like bread with Daniel. She was forty-four then. A change-of-life baby will break your heart, the old midwife told her. Two months before his due date Daniel was born in a tropical storm. He was her smallest baby but she'd had the worst time with him. She had all the others at the hospital but Daniel was born in her bed, bloody and breathless. Against her thigh, his skull was no larger than a monkey's, his skin translucent under the hurricane lanterns. The midwife wrapped him in a blanket and placed him in the drawer of a dresser. Carmelita had softened the edges of the drawer with cotton padding laid over sweet-smelling vetiver sprigs. For the first month of his life he wore a bracelet of black beads on his tiny wrist to ward off maljeaux while she prayed to keep the breath in his body. The baby had nothing of her flat, wide face and hairless sapodilla skin, or his father's smooth cocoa complexion. He was thin-faced with marmalade eyes, an amber-eyed throwback, a beautiful changeling child.

Father Duncan comes right behind Myrtle early on Saturday morning. Daniel has been gone three mornings. Four nights her son has slept somewhere else and she has no idea where. The night before, she'd not slept well, her feet aching from the long walk up the hill, and she rose twice in the night to the sound of a baby's cry. But each time it was only the big jumbie bird, roosting in the mango vert tree up behind the house. By time she waved Myrtle out the gate and turned to go back inside, Father Duncan is already striding up her path, as if tragedy has made him lose his manners, his crucifix glinting in the sun, his great head bobbing above the scarlet flowers of the hibiscus hedge. She has to hide Ganesh, snatching him from beside Jesus, pushing his elephant head deep in the compost heap. But in the end, she is happy the priest has come and they say the rosary together, pausing after each decade to allow the words to drift up to Mary's ears.

Beaubrun telephones on Monday morning.

"A body of a young boy was picked up by the Caura River.

They've sent him to the mortuary in town. That's all I know."

Her heart beats a galloping staccato that rushes in her ears and brings black spots before her eyes. The telephone falls from her hand and hits the statue of Mary, knocking the mother of God off her pedestal and narrowly missing the Sacred Heart with the bloody heart of Jesus popping out of his chest. Carmelita opens her mouth and bawls.

Afterwards she remembers that the village poured through her door like red ants, laying their hands on her, but even the softest touch bit and stung her skin and made her scream. It was only when old Dr. Chin arrived in his Honda CRV to stick a needle into her arm that Carmelita stopped screaming.

On Tuesday morning she packs a small bag to go to the mortuary. In it is a rosary, a bottle of holy water, a clean shirt and an ironed pair of pants for Daniel. Mr. Ali comes when she calls, holding her elbow as she walks to the car as if she is an old woman.

"You don't have to go with Mr. Ali, Ma," Johnny had said, "I'll take you."

But she had told him no. This was about her and Daniel.

The old colonial-built hospital is filled with airy rooms that filter the trade winds; the view through the jalousies looks down on vendors selling colas and fruit drinks at the entrance. At the back of the hospital, the mortuary stares at Carmelita, its closed windows giving it a stupid, blind appearance. Inside, a small Indian woman listens to Carmelita's story before picking up the telephone. As she speaks, a small extra finger swings gently from the side of her left hand. This infant finger with its own half-moon nail causes a somersaulting in Carmelita's stomach, a clenching in her womb. Across the room a wooden door bears the nameplate: Dr. Andrew Olivierre, Chief Pathologist. She takes a seat on a wooden bench across from this door.

"You can go in now," says the secretary.

Dr. Olivierre comes to meet as she walks through the door, holding out his hand and smiling pleasantly.

"I'm sorry," he says. "There has been a mistake. I'm so sorry, Mrs. Nunes."

"Excuse me?" Carmelita is confused. "The police sent me."

"We've seen this happen. People come in thinking they will find missing people here. But your son is not here."

They sit in silence for a moment or two. There is a picture of a pretty woman with three children on his desk. The woman looks like her daughter Oriana, same dark hair and wide mouth. The doctor has two sons and a daughter. The boy looks a little younger than Daniel and there is a baby in the woman's arms. The doctor flips his pen between his fingers and snaps it open and shut with sharp clicking noises.

"How you lose someone?" she asks the room. "A boy is not a handbag. Or a scrap of paper that fly off a table and disappear in the breeze; a boy is not something you could lose so."

"I'm so sorry for your loss, Mrs. Nunes," the doctor says, his hand resting lightly between her shoulders as she leaves the room.

She waits on the bench outside the hospital for Johnny to come and get her. She still has the bag of Daniel's clothes and the small bottle of holy water.

That night she dreams that Father Duncan caught a scarlet ibis and asked her to stew it for him to eat. The next morning, Wednesday, she draws a black line through the whole week on her almanac. She chooses a picture of Daniel sitting with the two dogs on her front porch. She will go back and give the doctor a picture. If Daniel does come in, at least he will recognize him.

When the car pulls in to the mortuary the next morning, Carmelita is waiting. The doctor is in the passenger seat. The dark-haired woman from the picture kisses him good-bye, waving as he walks away.

"Goodbye," she calls.

The morning sun backlights the doctor's hair, but his face turns mulish and cruel as he approaches Carmelita. Still, she reaches out to touch him. When he clamps her wrist, she remembers a dog had bitten her like this once, with a sudden snap.

"Your son is not here," he says, his big body, with its womanish bottom, stiff and hostile.

Behind him, the car stops, its engine idling, in the middle of the road.

"Drew!" the woman calls.

Carmelita pulls her hand back, shaking her wrist, the photograph falling on the ground. When she looks up he has walked away and the big car had driven off.

Drew

Drew carefully examined the body of the young boy. He had been brought in after midnight early Sunday morning. Blue and black discolourations of settling blood were just starting along the boy's back, his skin grey under the buzzing fluorescent lights. Tall, but still a child. No more than sixteen or seventeen. Could be a country boy, a cocoa panyol mixed with some Indian. There was a birthmark on his left cheek. Maybe a local white, but Drew doubted this because he'd know this child. Venezuelan? His mouth had collapsed into the spaces left by the missing front teeth, making the boy's face appear babyish. Drew turned up the top lip. The gums were bruised, puckering around little bloody pockets left by the extracted teeth. Drew ran his tongue over his own front teeth, a quick reflexive move. The ends of the boy's fingers had bled until death and now the hands curled lightly, peculiar and birdlike without their nails. Even with closed eyes, his face still had the startled expression of a panicked child as if the bullet had caught him negotiating to the end. A drug hit? But Drew knew that if Ralph had called him out, it meant the police were involved.

After he'd examined the body, Drew peeled his surgical gloves off, discarding them in the bin. The yellow death certificates came in triplicate, untidy with their bulging carbon copies. On the top copy, Drew carefully wrote the cause of death as vehicular accident. Underneath, he signed his name: Dr. Andrew Olivierre, Chief Pathologist, St. Mary's General Hospital.

The first bodies had begun arriving within weeks of the election. Last week there'd been a prostitute, a pretty girl who had tried to blackmail the wrong person. Was Ralph so powerful that he could arbitrarily order someone to be killed? Drew pulled the sheet up, covering the child's face. Where were this boy's parents? They were the ones to blame for this. He could put his head on a block that none of his three would ever end up like this. Irresponsible people having children had spawned a generation of feral teenagers. This is what the ruling party had said during the election campaign and the population had agreed so much that the party had swept into government on a landslide vote.

At his weekly confession, Drew had struggled with his conscience. What was he to say to the priest? That part of his job as the government pathologist was to make the victims of police brutality disappear? It was not as if he were associated with a death squad or anything like the Ton Ton Macoute in Haiti. This was simply some housecleaning to tidy up the streets. He turned off the lights, locked the door and left. It was 3.15 am on Sunday morning. The boy had been dead for a little over twenty-four hours.

Ralph and Drew still met every Wednesday at the Cricket Club, even though Ralph was now a government minister. When they had turned up for lunch that first Wednesday after the election, the whole room had stood and clapped when Ralph entered. He looked like a Minister of National Security, as if everything in his life had been leading up to playing this part. Drew had held his briefcase while Ralph stopped to shake hands with people on the way to their table.

But today, no one had looked up when they entered the room.

Drew cut his chicken carefully as he spoke. "The mother tried to stop me in the car park this morning. I told her we didn't have him. We should have buried him on Monday."

"Does anyone else know he was brought in?" asked Ralph.

"I should ask *you* that. This was a child. Shit man. This is not what we're supposed to be doing."

"What a fuck up. We didn't know he was so young." Ralph sipped his drink. "We think he double-crossed Jamiah."

"I still don't understand. Who killed the boy?"

"Our men did. He knew everything about Jamiah but he couldn't go back. We offered him protection to talk, but he refused."

"We can't be killing children."

"You know the little shit never cracked. He never talked."

"They were very rough with him," said Drew. This is where I should say something, he thought, this is where I should get up and walk out.

"This boy doesn't exist any more, so whoever 'they' are, could not have been rough with him. Do you understand? This boy must disappear completely. This was a fucking nightmare and now you giving me some crap to hold about this boy's mother? Make him disappear, Drew. It's your job."

No, Drew wanted to say, it's not my job. This was not supposed to be part of it.

"How long we go back, Drew? Come nah man. How long we friends?"

"I'd like you to be part of my team," Ralph had said.

How many months ago? Was it six already?

"If we want to clean up this country, we have to bend the rules a bit."

He'd presented a convincing argument, but Drew had always known that he didn't have a choice.

In their final year at university, Drew had listened most nights to Ralph's low voice cajoling and stroking, the murmurs travelling through the walls. He couldn't believe the girls fell for it. But they did, every time. With a fleshy mouth that glistened pink and healthy when he laughed, a booming hahaha mouth that opened to show big, white teeth and a small, pointed tongue, Ralph was beautiful.

"It's not whether I like him or not. It's not about that. You can't resist Ralph, he's like a force of nature," Drew told Isobel when he first started seeing her.

"I can resist him," she said.

"That's what all women say," he told her, but secretly he was pleased that she could see through Ralph.

Was this how it happened? That you crossed lines so easily? On their small island, where good and evil were so carefully demarcated, it was surprisingly easy to move between the two. Ralph was supported by a strong religious platform. It had been a clever manoeuvre by their Prime Minister to appeal to the righteous, a hardnosed approach that sent shivers around the region. What was it the papers around the region said? An unprecedented show of military muscle.

Every day, from the window in his office, Drew looked at the palms that waved the dead through, large branches forming a canopy against the sun. He was sorry that he had met with the boy's mother; sorry that she'd shown him the picture of the boy. In the photograph, an even-featured boy with odd topaz eyes had smiled out at him. White teeth set against copper skin, a saga-boy smile.

"Why do they keep calling you out at night?" Isobel had asked him on the way to work that morning. "Tell Ralph, when you have lunch with him today, that your wife wants to know why he keeps calling her husband in the middle of the night."

That night, after they'd made love, Isobel fell asleep with her back pressed up against him. She was sleeping deeply when he shook her awake.

"I have something to tell you," he said.

Isobel

The night Drew had woken her to tell her about the boy there was no more lovemaking. She had taken a sleeping pill to fall asleep again. She woke groggy and waited for him to go to work before she got up. The hot water beating on her head when she showered cleared her thoughts. She would find the boy's mother and tell her the terrible thing her husband had done. She wore a comfortable pair of shoes; it would take an hour to walk to the hospital where she guessed the woman would be. Drew had taken the car that morning and he would be expecting her to stay at home.

She walked through the cows that grazed under the branches of the large saman trees. The passion fruit vine on the fence that separated their house from the banking complex was heavy with fragrant globes. She walked past the guava trees on the hillock that overlooked the houses of the rich on the coast. From here she could see the hospital on the other side of the savannah, up the street and left off the highway. She timed her breath to her stride, as if she were pacing herself for a long run. The road was quiet, the school rush over, her girls sitting safely in their classrooms; Robbie was having his morning fruit at his grandmother's home. Behind her, a truck roared up the highway, gears grinding as it picked up speed. She walked faster trying to outpace the memory of Drew's face. He dropped the children to school every morning, letting her sleep because he knew she liked to read late into the night. He'd probably kept them quiet this morning, packing Robby's bag and putting Mara's hair in a ponytail.

She broke into a short run, her breath labouring, as the truck thundered past her, leaving her with a lungful of diesel fumes.

The woman was where she expected. She'd noticed her a few days before, the day she'd dropped Drew to work. She'd seen the violence in the way he'd grabbed the woman's hand. This had so shocked Isobel, she'd braked the car and called out to him. Now it made sense. And this was how she knew the woman would be here, sitting on a bench outside the mortuary.

They have him, Isobel said when she sat down next to the boy's mother. They have him inside. I'll come with you to get him. Come we will go together. She was ready to face Drew. There was no need to tell the woman what had happened; she would be given a sealed casket. She told Carmelita to say that she would return with a lawyer if they did not produce her son. Drew let them into his office, his face even. Had she expected something more dramatic, a scene perhaps or some form of repentance? Instead his quiet acquiescence frightened her. She'd been sure that she had the upper hand, but she'd underestimated him and now it was she who was forced to consider her position. What had she gambled with this move, what must she be prepared to surrender?

The casket is sealed, he told Carmelita. These discrepancies are quite normal. We were due to call you today. I am so sorry for your loss.

Isobel was thrown by his poise, shocked by his ability to lie so easily. This shifting of gears revealed a stranger hidden inside her husband. When she was a child, she'd once slept

25

the whole night with a garden lizard under the blanket. It had made her feel ill to think of the lizard heating up from her warmth.

The casket will go to the funeral home, she heard him say, I'm signing the papers to release the body to the funeral home. You can bury him from there.

When he came home that evening, they did not speak for three days. On the third night, he woke her in the middle of the night.

"Do you know what the fuck you have done?" he asked her. "Do you? You've put us all in danger."

"I don't want to know, Drew." She kept her face averted. How much was she prepared to give up? Her marriage? The lives of her children?

The next morning they went on as usual because neither could think of what else to do.

It was only later that Isobel was able to piece together what had happened. The woman had bribed the funeral director to release the casket to her.

"Let me bring the boy home for a last night. Let me feed his spirit one last meal. Let me pack his bag for heaven."

This is what Isobel imagined Carmelita would have said to the funeral director. It's what she would have said.

Later Carmelita told her that she had bathed Daniel with lavender-scented water, sponging each laceration and examining every inch of his body. The next morning, she'd asked Father Duncan to reseal his coffin. In the family plot, he settled gently in the loamy dirt grown by generations of flesh and blood. That night, Carmelita had found a gun hidden under some clothes in Daniel's room. There was no one that she could ask about the technicalities of a gun. It shot when she fired. She'd looked up the address of Dr.

Andrew Olivierre. It had taken her less than a week to learn the man's routine.

★

It still surprised Isobel that neither child had mentioned the attack at the old house. In the aftermath, both girls had been calm. Carmelita had appeared just after midday. The neighbours said she had sat there for most of the afternoon, waiting through a light drizzle under the trunk of a frangipani tree. When Drew pulled up to the gate, she moved quickly. When she heard the first shots Isobel ran towards the echo. By the time she arrived at the gate, Drew had Carmelita pinned against the car. With her arm twisted behind her back, her scapula stood in bold relief, like a broken wing.

Isobel pulled Drew off the keening woman, her hands frantic over his body, feeling for mortal wounds to explain the blood.

Surface wounds, she told him. It's okay. It's okay, Drew. It's just a pellet gun. It's just pellets. Isobel knew that old women who live in the hills knew how to deliver babies, brew raw medicine, and cook like angels, but they did not know how to use guns. The pellet gun had wobbled in her trembling hands.

"Why you lie? Why you lie about Daniel? You know they kill him. You see how they strip his body and rip it up like a old bed sheet. You see how they knock out his teeth and pull out his nails. I grow that child like a plant. From a seed, I grow him. Why you lie, Mr. Doctor? God don't sleep. You will rot in hell."

"Stop it," said Isobel. "Enough."

"Miss Isobel. Is his signature. His writing. He signed it. And he had to see what I saw. He knew. He knew what they did and he lied for them. Is pure evil. Pure evil that your husband do that night."

27

That night Isobel and Drew made love for the first time since the day she'd appeared with Carmelita. At first they were cautious but soon they held each other with the sharp bites and blind thrusts of an unsettled argument. They were still very good together. But that morning she kept her face averted, throwing an arm over her eyes and turning inward until he left the bed, not wanting to see the scabby marks on his chest.

By the end of the week they had moved to a quiet suburb and changed their phone numbers.

★

Isobel had never lived in the shadow of a mahogany tree. It stood tall, reaching towards the sky, giving off resinous clicks as it stretched its branches over the house. In the evening, the tree turned its leaves to catch the dry season breeze that rode down the valley. If she listened from the kitchen, Isobel could hear the tiny pops as the tree released its cocoa-shaped pods, setting free the little helicopter-spirals. Each morning she collected the spent husks where they lay curled like tiny sculptures on the sloping lawn that ran to the edge of the driveway.

The man who had lived there many years before had raised hibiscus. People had driven from all corners of the island to choose from his rainbow-hued hybrids. It gave her pleasure to return hibiscus to the garden and tuck them neatly into fat, manure beds that she shaped with her garden hoe.

Her new home was deceptive, modestly folding in on itself, presenting a bland façade to the road, but it came from a long pedigree of high-ceilinged, graceful houses that dotted the surrounding hills. It was not like the home of the man who lived across the street, a good-looking brown-skin man they nicknamed 'The whistler'. His house was con-temporary, spare-boned, dramatic.

Below their house was a damp cellar, secured with a temperamental padlock, where Isobel stored the baby bassinet with its elaborate netting and faint scent of vetiver. She had spent her first mornings in their new home in this cool dark cave rooting out hidden treasures from long-gone eras. All the while she hunted, she could hear her neighbour whistling his way through a catchy series of 1920's dance hits. She heard him sweeping his front-steps as he whistled, a cheerful reassuring sound that reminded her of the nursery smell of boiling rice and butter. When she'd looked out from the cellar, all she could see was the smudge of his broom as it danced in a mist of sunlit dust motes. She'd heard that he was very rich, money made from growing tomatoes, according to the other neighbours.

Isobel and Drew seldom spoke of the incident at the old house. Now days were spent arranging new routines. Once she had built her world on the assumption that Drew was a good man. It was he who attended church with the three children every week. Her oldest, at eight, had just begun to question why Isobel came only infrequently to mass. Ava was pretty and fine-boned, looking like Drew's mother, and the old lady shamelessly favoured her over the younger and plumper Mara. Her baby, Robert, was still beautiful in a bow-lipped, milky way. Everyone had told her that she would love the third child the most. When he emerged, perfectly whole and male, she feared he would steal her heart from her daughters. But her love for each child had a distinct flavour and texture, mercurial in the way it bubbled through her life.

The new house sat in the shadow of the whistler's house. At certain times of the day, the rawboned house eclipsed their light, blocking the sun at its hottest point. Ralph had found the house for them after the shooting, though for a time there was talk about moving to Canada. Ralph said not to worry about Carmelita and they had not pressed charges. There would be no retribution and even if she did go to the police, she would not get far. Isobel made Drew promise that Ralph would not harm the old lady.

"It's the least you can do for her."

Ralph said he knew the neighbour, a nice man. He grew lots of tomatoes; he'd made his fortune in them. When she'd first heard him whistling, Isobel had thought about the boy. That day, on the bench outside the mortuary, Carmelita had told Isobel about Daniel. In his last months, Daniel had learned to whistle. He perfected the birdcalls of the northern range, practising the gong sound of the bell-bird that lived high in the moist forest, and whistling out of the window at the jumbie bird in the mango tree. These were memories Carmelita wanted to keep.

It was good that Carmelita and Isobel never knew the bloody tune Daniel whistled until the end. Or how the soldiers in the forest had prepared the body of the child in the way that they were taught by their elders. Brutal as they had been in life, they were gentle and superstitious in death, preparing the body with deference, worrying about the nine-night's ritual. Should they send a note to Dr. Drew to ask him to nail the boy's feet to the hastily assembled box that guilt made them build before they sent him to the mortuary? Should they insist that Dr. Drew bury the boy face down so he could not come back for retribution? In their heavy uniforms, these men did not fear the living, but deep in the forest they would take no chances with a dead boy.

If Isobel had known these things, she might not have stayed. But she never knew any of this. Instead, in the dry rotting-leaf smell of her new garden, she learned how to skim unwelcome thoughts from the surface of her mind.

It was Mara who saw the dragonfly, a big blue darner among the red ones who gathered every evening to dance above the olive water of the pond. Did you know, Isobel whispered, tickling the girls, old wives say that he uses his tail to sew the lips of naughty boys shut? The devil's darning needles. They'd looked for him again, but he'd only come that once.

THE GAYELLE

In the night the water rose. It rose until the littoral was no more.
It rose until the savannahs forgot the footprints of men and learned
instead to mould themselves around the fish that poured into the
dragon's boca. The animals left adrift on the block of land stared
for a long time. From where the jaguar and the anteater stood, the
land did not seem so different to the Orinoco Valley. It was only
the people who cried, stretching their hands to the mainland.

Benita stands parallel to the window. Her body carves a dark
silhouette against the outside light, her long neck like a
funnel leading down to into her belly that holds the baby. If
her son Mannie squints and looks through shielded eyes, he
imagines it floating – womb-bound only by the thick cord
that his mother grows to anchor what burgeons within.

"If you fight the cock, it will lose." She makes this
declaration with finality.

It has come to this because it is now February and the
roosters have stopped their moulting. Soon the path to the
gayelle will be smooth and dry; the handlers, thin men like
his father, will squat around the pen while the roosters jump
and stab with their spurs. In the second week of February,
the weather shape-shifts in the night. All along the island,
thick rivers drink the sea and at night glow blue under the
moon. When they visit his mother's family on the banks of
the Ortoire River, sometimes Mannie swims in the brown

river, throwing the water into the air, beads spreading their inflorescence into the night.

His father had a wife before his mother, but she died in childbed. When Mannie first heard this term, he imagined his father's first wife climbing into a small bed and dying. As if tiny pillows and soft blankets could choke a grown woman. It was only later that he understood that the babies killed her as they pushed their way to air. They tore her up like an old bed sheet, he heard his mother whisper to his aunt. There had been two; two babies that lived for less than a week. His father's wife had bled out on the bed.

When his mother came, driving herself in the red truck, the tray packed with suitcases, aloe plants, and a ram goat, she'd insisted that the room be blessed before she stepped foot in the house. His father had burnt the bed. The first wife was buried in the big cemetery in Mayaro, the one that ran beside the road cresting the hill as you rounded the blind corner, coming out of the forest and moving away from the river. Here she lay, her grave not yet flat but still mounded with soil that is only just begun to lose its freshness, even though it is nine years old, one year older than Mannie. Sometimes, when they visit, the grave has been decorated with the bright red canna lilies that grow wild in the swampy mud of the coast. She was very beautiful, his father's first wife, and her mother is said to be comforted that her daughter can hear the waves when the tide is in. Mannie's mother, Benita, is also very beautiful. Some say she is more beautiful than her cousin but Mannie cannot say because there are no photographs of his father's first wife.

The babies lie under the silk cotton trees on the Sangre Chiquito estate, just out of line of sight of the house. Mannie's father dug the graves himself. How Mannie knows these things he cannot say. The stories grow with him, stretching and changing as easily as his skin.

Benita turns her head to look out the window. She is waiting for her mother and sisters to come from Manzanilla. They will wash baby clothes and prepare the room for the new baby. When Benita turns, her torso follows a second later, sluggish in the heat. Her hair is held with two turtle-shell clips. Mannie has never seen his mother's hair loose but he knows from the strands that he finds in her small-toothed comb that each strand is long and fine, the shiny black of cockroach wings. His grandfather made the combs. His grandmother gave them to his mother when she was sent to replace her dead cousin. He didn't think his mother minded too much. He's overheard her talking to her sisters when they come to visit Sangre Chiquito and lie in her bed all afternoon, laughing and rubbing her feet. She whispers things to them that make them laugh and cover their mouths and she shushes them when he comes into the room.

Mannie's father is a small, fair-complexioned man, more Spanish than Indian and he is not old. He is proud that he carries the blood of the Warao tribe and he makes the crossing from Cedros to the mainland once or twice a year. When he comes back to them he is laden with all manner of mainland novelties: packages of queso blanco, giant peewah, palm hammocks, scarlet macaws and, sometimes, a fighting rooster. On those days he is clothed in importance but today he wears a stained pair of khaki shorts and a white merino vest. Three beads of blood spot his freshly shaved jawline. His parents share a razor, an old fashioned silver thing without a safety guard.

When Benita's sisters and mother come, Mannie's father leaves and goes to the chickens, but Mannie stays because he likes to be close to his mother. He is still a little boy. Soon the women try to guess the sex of the baby. Someone hangs a wedding ring on a piece of red ribbon and swings it gently in front of her stomach. First the ring spins from side to side. A girl, they shout. But then the ring begins to swing in large lazy circles, not unlike a dowsing pendulum, picking up speed until it bumps Benita and slowly stops spinning. Twins! All the women make the sign of the cross but Benita says nothing.

Some nights Benita dreams of her dead cousin; she dreams they are children again swimming in the big cistern next to her father's house in Manzanilla. Benita dreams the water is cold and green and her cousin breaks the surface face up, her long hair streaming behind her. When Benita dreams this dream, she wonders if Mannie remembers the day the water swallowed him.

Mannie remembers Benita picking him up out of his crib and bringing him to lie in the hammock on the verandah. The breeze from the sea had been constant, the coconut tree branches above forming a cocoon of sound. You cannot remember, Benita has told him. It's impossible. You were barely walking. You were only three. But he does remember. He even remembers the tiny cross around her neck that later sank to the bottom of the cistern. She'd put him in the hammock after lunch, rocking him slowly as he drifted to sleep in the breeze.

I saw the water at the end of the floor, he told her. Where the floor ends, the water looked as if it was walking towards me. I thought I saw you calling me. You were standing on the water.

Later when Benita lay in the hammock and tried to see with baby eyes, it did seem as if the cistern ran off the edge of the verandah, the water hyacinths coming up like torches from the surface. What did I look like? She'd asked him this many times over the years. Like you but different. Thinner. Whiter. What did I sound like? Like you. You sounded like you.

Mannie had rocked in the hammock watching his mother go back into the drawing room. She was not far. From where he lay, the coconut trees on his grandfather's land seemed to stand on the water, and he was sure the calm un-punctured expanse was as solid as the blanket under him. In the calm, suspended state between waking and sleep, when he sucked his thumb and hummed, the vibration in his mouth moved to the top of his head and became part of the slide into unconsciousness, his world turning green, then luminous. When he woke on that day in late June, he was hot. Someone was calling him. A woman at the end of the verandah was standing on the water calling him softly. He slipped out of the hammock and unclipped the black latch on the gallery gate as he had seen his mother do many times before. He thought it was Benita and he went to her eagerly. From the gate it was only a few feet to the deep end of the cistern and towards the woman standing on the water.

It was a great shock to him that the surface of the water was not solid and that the woman was not Benita. He sank in slow motion, opening his mouth to cry, but the water rushed in and clogged his lungs. He did not yet know of things like abalones and clams, fish or eels, but in the deep green of fresh water he thought he saw things that he would later come to know as things of the deep sea.

Benita was boiling a pot of zebapique, stripping and crushing the bitter leaves, when she heard the latch of the gate. A winnow of air brought the sound of ruptured water straight to her belly. It resonated as a vibration, a sense of something changing in the air of the house. When Benita ran to Mannie, he was lying on the bottom of the cistern, glowing like the inside of a shell. Wailing, Benita broke the surface with Mannie's limp body and laid him under the green canopy of overhanging ferns. Her mother brought herbs while Benita breathed life into the limp lungs, pumping the baby chest and feeling the fingerling ribs under her palms. When Mannie began coughing, Benita keened and keened over his wet head.

Mannie's father was deep in the forest fighting roosters.

The next day Benita and her mother drove the pick-up to Moruga to visit the woman who walked barefoot through the forest.

"It's the roosters," the woman said.

Benita's cousin had fought the roosters with Mannie's father. Together they had groomed the birds, training them with zeal to be winners. Benita had seen her cousin wrap her long mane of hair around Mannie's father's neck and kiss him hard on the mouth after a win. These are things that Benita remembers.

"You must make him stop fighting the roosters. It is the idle spilling of blood." The woman from Moruga gave them bags of leaves and bowls of blue soap. She told them the dead cousin would concede on many things but not the roosters. "Blood will call blood. He must stop now."

On the way back to Manzanilla, Benita and her mother bought a small white hen. At home in Sangre Chiquito the next day, Benita slit the hen's throat and bled it out across the path to the coop.

Beyond the window of the small bungalow, silk cottons, immortelles, pouis, and teak stagger their way down to the river. In the dry season, the season of the fighting, the leaves fall and fall until they settle ankle-deep in rustling layers.

Benita says that below the leaves lies not just hard earth but the pineapple backs of sleeping mapepires and the pale brown of scorpions. At the beginning of each year, Benita collects scorpions, hunting them under rotten logs and behind abandoned tools before roasting them. She feeds the ground paste to Mannie, blowing in his face to stop him gagging. This way, she says, he will not die if he is stung by the lightning strike of a curved tail.

Two babies slipped from her womb after Mannie. He knows that his mother blames her cousin, the beautiful first wife, lying in her grave, listening to the sea and wanting placenta-grown babies. Mannie grows and the roosters continue to fight but Benita is ever vigilant. She has learned many things from the woman in Moruga. She has learned how to make Mannie's father love her until he whispers Benita Benita into her neck until they sleep; she has learned how to brew potions that help keep her dead cousin quiet in the ground.

On the day her cousin died, nine Februaries gone, a champion cock, the last of a Spanish line, had fought his last. Now Mannie's father trains the roosters where his wife cannot see, and when she walks outside she avoids the path that leads to the coop. Recently, Mannie has joined his father.

With the roosters, his father is gentle. He weighs them, meticulously recording the weight of each bird on a chart he tapes to the bare brick walls of the shed. There are ten new ones, five pullets and five stags. It is the stags that will take up most of his father's time as he grooms them into roosters. Some are belligerent and aggressive, some are courtly, almost gentlemanly. The tradition has come down five generations, Mannie's father tells him proudly. In Venezuela and Puerto Rico they still fight the roosters. They understand the importance of tradition. The rooster that will fight on Sunday has won many competitions – a noble creature. Now his father is handing him over to Mannie. They will fight their first fight on Sunday in the gayelle.

On the morning of the fight, Benita finds the shattered shells of water crabs, the red manicou crabs that come from the mountain rivers.

"Do not go," she tells Mannie's father. "I am pregnant with twins."

When he continues to pack the cages, Benita makes Mannie bathe with the thin foam from the blue balls that the Moruga woman gave her. Then she untangles her mother's chaplet and places it around Mannie's neck.

The champion is plumed, crested, and combed with a keen eye. His father shows Mannie how to clip feathers with a small scissors, how to shave the tiny pinfeathers from the fine legs of the bird so that when it strikes there will be no drag on the air. After he trains the birds at the height of noon, Mannie's father rubs their legs with bay rum to cool their blood. Their champion has been training for months; swimming in the barrel, running on the wheel. He has never lost a fight. His father teaches him to stroke the birds so they lie quiet and relaxed, dazed and sleepy, their spurs at ease.

At the gayelle the handlers squat in the dust. Over in the far corner are the Venezuelans who have come with their birds. Look at their hats, says his father. The men wear peculiar triangle-shaped hats that Mannie has never seen before. The men under the hats have hard, lined faces and smoke with cigarettes balancing in the corners of their mouths. Their roosters lie panting and leashed in the shade of the forest trees. To get into the gayelle, they must pass a man who only lets them in when they whisper the secret word.

From the beginning Mannie can tell his rooster is in trouble. He is in the pen with a Venezuelan bird and Mannie knows there is a lot of money riding on each spurred kick. The skin under their bird's throat opens suddenly, like a third eye. Mannie enters the ring and handles the bird gently, taping the wound before coming out of the ring to squat silently next to his father. With each flap and kick, their rooster goes back in for more and Mannie's father begins to cry soundlessly.

Mannie's rooster begins to die before them. His father cries openly and the rooster is limp in the ring. From the opposite side, the Venezuelan handler moves in to retrieve his champion. Mannie must walk into the ring and collect the bundle of feathers and the dimming eyes.

It is night by the time they arrive home, his father still weeping silently behind the wheel of the red Frontier, the dead rooster in a box on Mannie's lap. The road in the forest twists to the left before entering the clearing where their bungalow is set back from the forest's edge. To the right, his mother's goat looks out of his pen and the pack of pot hounds that follow his mother everywhere run out into the headlights of the truck, barking and jumping in and out of the beams of light that sweep across the dark house. When Mannie is an old man, his children will tell him it is impossible for the river to send her blue water to the forest. But Mannie will remember the beads of blue luminescence, the drizzle of sapphire that rained gently on the house when his father stepped out of the truck, calling and calling for his mother, leaving Mannie with the dead rooster in the box on his lap.

When Mannie comes into the kitchen, his mother is

cooking by the light of the kerosene lamp. His father has pulled the combs out and is hiding his tears in Benita's hair, twisting it around his face and neck. On the stove, the roosters bubble in their fragrant broth. There is a pot on each of the four burners of his mother's new stove. As the roosters stew, she holds herself under her belly, supporting the heads of the babies that want to fall.

THE HAT

Somewhere in San Rafael, in the centre of the island, Chale sits in the front seat of the small black car waiting to kidnap a woman. The woman's name is Maria Estella and that is all he knows. He takes his instructions from Dougla who is sitting in the back of the sedan. While they wait, Chale drums a tune on the steering wheel to pass the time. He's only just turned seventeen but last year Dougla paid for the licence tucked in the back pocket of his jeans. The car is parked off the main road, under the teak trees that run to the clearing of razor grass. The house sits at the end of a winding bridle path and the woman's car is parked so that it is not visible from the main road. In the ashy dusk, the fruit bats swoop under the mango trees before fanning out into the forest.

While he waits for the signal from Dougla, Chale idly unpacks the glove compartment: three lipsticks melted and ruined by the daytime heat in the car, an insurance certificate, and a wedding invitation. The sedan belongs to a woman they held up in Curepe last night. Moving up the ranks, Dougla told him. Now Chale opens the door of the car and steps out into the chill evening air. Carefully and slowly he makes his way down the hill and around the back of the house. He must knock on the door at precisely 6.45 pm. June evenings run long and he must pick the moment when it is neither day nor night.

Through a Demerara window at the back of the house Chale can see Maria Estella soundlessly counting as she places the cash in tidy packets, each secured with a pink rubber-band. She places each packet neatly in a suitcase lying open on the wooden floor in front of her. The room is bare except for two chairs and a long dining-room table. Above the table, a chandelier sways gently in the evening breeze and moth shadows grow with the dusk. One side of the room is already in darkness.

"Come boy, time to move." Chale says to himself.

Maria Estella comes to the door with the first knock. He smiles at her through the window, raising his hand to his mouth as if he wants to ask her a question. He has deliberately made his face slack and pleasant. In the moment it takes for her to look away, her face frowning with worry, her hand reaching to slide another lock, he has gotten through the door. When he pushes her hard, she goes down quickly. With his hands on her shoulders, he straddles her. His jeans slip and slide on her shirt as he bounces on her chest. Between his thighs, she is solid and he comes down hard on her, squeezing until he feels the outline of rib under the flesh. With each bounce she exhales little puffs of air, blowing into his face a woman smell that must come from deep inside. Keep calm, he tells himself. You can do this.

When he raises his hand to push her she misunderstands the gesture, thinking there is something behind her that he wants to hit, perhaps a moth or a bat. When he pushes her, she is surprised to find herself down, weak from fright and anger, the back of her head slamming into the wooden floor. There are three locks on the door. She thinks how angry the man will be that they were not all latched. Within seconds, the boy has straddled her, climbing onto her as if she is a bicycle. Her heart thuds until she can't catch her breath and she sucks desperately for air, her ribs straining against the weight of his thighs, her shirt sliding under his jeans. Behind his head she can see another man coming through the door. It's happened so fast, she's caught somewhere between detachment and panic; the keening takes a few seconds to come. She hears it as if from a distance; a sound unrelated to her voice. It stops when the boy spreads five fingers across her mouth, star-fishing the centre of her face.

"Cool yourself," says the other man to the boy, cool and calm. "You don't need to fuck up now."

She turns on her stomach, panicked and wailing, kicking back hard, her mouth spilling an odd bird cry.

In the car she tells herself, Calm down, calm down. Pay attention to where they are driving. In pulling her down the stairs, they hurt her back and now it pulses in little angry spasms. The man drives and the boy sits in the back with her, his hand resting lightly on her head, keeping her under the blanket they have used to conceal her. She worries that she will suffocate so she lies quietly and paces her breathing. They drive for a long time, turning sharp corners until she is dizzy and carsick. When the car stops, there is the smell of night forest and the hum and chirrup of tree frogs.

It is only when they make her walk through the forest that Maria Estella cries for the first time, her childhood terror of snakes rushing back. She thinks they are somewhere in the Guayaguayare forest, heading east. She remembers all the stories she's heard of hunting dogs dying from the bite of the mapepires that hide under rotting logs. Soon she is sweating, breathing heavily, trying to map where they are going. The boy who walks in front of her is young. His hair is long and she can tell it has been a few days since he has washed it. It is oily but combed and straight, parting randomly and exposing the yellow skin on his skull and the tender lines of his ear cartilage, delicate as an agouti. He keeps looking back at her. As her eyes grow accustomed to the underwater light of the moon, she sees the dougla man has his gun trained on the boy as well. She walks on a leash between the two men, the older, heavier man bringing up the rear. By the time they stop, her feet are stinging and bleeding, her toes stumped and sore. They tie her to a pole in a pit latrine and bring a bottle of water and a tin bucket. She grew up in a house with a pit latrine and the smell takes her back to the little hut above the river. This latrine is a cocktail of different shit. There is the frothy smell of diarrhoea and she hopes she does not get sick. They leave her blindfolded, her hands tied behind her back.

That night Maria Estella thinks about her mother's house above the scattering of board houses on the Arima-Blanchisseuse road, surrounded by forest trees with names that she likes to roll on her tongue, imagining the texture of a bark: the pain d'epice and the cajuca; the bois canot and the balata. They grew up near the river, away from the spiny brush of the coast. She remembers the sound of the river after rain in its hurry to get to the sea. She senses there is a river nearby and when it rains sometime after midnight, she can hear the water rushing, adding to the sound of the surf, which cannot be far. From underneath the old piece of galvanize that is the door, a sea breeze mixes with a rain breeze and makes her think of her mother.

"Don't mind, auntie," Chale had said. "We'll take off the blindfold in the morning. Kick the bucket when you want to pee. You hear? Don't make a mistake and pee on the floor."

As if the floor is not already stinking and rank.

As an afterthought he leant in and whispered, a soussous sound hardly audible above the sound of the trees, "Or call me, call my name soft. It's Chale."

When her bladder stretches hard and tight, she feels with her foot for the bucket and kicks it until the Chale comes. He pulls her jeans and panties down and tells her to squat. She puts her hand on his shoulder to balance and smells the oil in his hair as the warm urine runs down the side of her leg, splattering into the tin bucket that the boy then pours into the latrine hole. After two days of peeing, the hole fills and stinks. By Sunday she can smell herself. The dougla man comes to visit, smelling of expensive cologne and cigar smoke. She can't imagine where he's made camp to be looking so clean. Perhaps Mayaro with its coconut trees and fancy beach houses is nearby.

"Just a little water, please," she tells him. "I'll tell him you treated me well. The man. I'll make sure he knows you treated me kindly. It will matter."

The dougla man looks at her for a long time before flicking ash into the bucket.

"You bathing for me, sweet thing?"

It is then that she is sure this is not a test. The dougla man has kidnapped her because he thinks he can outsmart the man, mistaking discretion for weakness. If they'd been real professionals they would have taken her north into the hilly northern range. It was the geographical move that made her think at first she was being tested. But now she realises it is merely stupidity and greed on the dougla man's part. By now, the man will have missed the money. He'll be looking for her. Looking for his suitcase.

For a moment, Maria Estella thinks the dougla man will rape her and for the first time she is truly frightened. Before this she has been angry, bent on retribution. But now, the dougla man's dumb, blunt features make it clear that he has no idea that there will be consequences for stealing both her and the suitcase. She knows that amateurs are the most dangerous. But there is no interest in the dougla's eyes. He could be someone she'd meet at a fete, looking just like thousands of Trinidadian men, no defining edge. He is brown skinned with a smooth, high forehead and the beginnings of a receding hairline. He doesn't look dangerous. A true true mix-up dougla. His mother might be Indian, his father black; maybe some Chinee in him. The kind of saga-boy her mother always liked and she bets there's a woman somewhere in the background. Men like this dougla man don't move without a woman for long. While he talks, Maria Estella lowers herself to sit with her back against the raw bricks of the latrine, her feet filthy and swollen.

She notices that the boy, Chale, does not take his eyes off the dougla man. The boy, thin and young, positions himself between her and the man.

"The man is going to pay the ransom." The man stands away from the latrine, throwing his voice like a stone. "You understand how these things work don't you?"

She does. But does he?

★

Sometimes, before the twins were born, rich people from Port of Spain would call for Maria Estella's mother to cook in their weekend homes on the Blanchisseuse coast. Maria Estella looked nothing like her mother. Her mother said she looked nothing like her father either. Maria Estella did not know whether this was so, because her father died as she was beginning her descent into the world. A hunting accident. His friend had mistaken him for a deer. When next her mother had grown big and round, the houses on the coast stopped sending for her.

Maria Estella had cut the birth cords on both her sisters, taking each placenta out into the yard in a Breeze laundry detergent bucket and burying them deep under the silk cotton tree in the backyard. She'd buried the little navel strings, stringy and twisted, on the other side of the tree. They must never forget where they've come from, her mother said, her legs still spread and bleeding, the twins huddling under their mother's arm like naked birds. The iron smell of blood stayed on Maria Estella's hands for days, mixed with the smell of baby shit and breast milk. She was ten and afraid that her mother would die and leave her with the mewling babies.

Maria Estella was a panyol bred on a cocoa estate high in the northern range. Like any sport grown in the rain forest, she emerged with talents exceeding either parent. Born with the caul over her face, she had a peculiar sallowness that radiated off her skin as a tender green that eventually settled in the corners of her mouth and around her eyes. When she showed her gift, it was an unusual one for a young girl: an uncanny ability to understand how the business worked. With little effort, she mapped in her head the routes between Peru, Bolivia, and Colombia, how they funnelled into ever smaller channels via ship or light plane until destination zero was reached – the metropolis where rich white people were willing to pay big money for altered states. The man taught her about the Golden Crescent, the heroin routes that ran out of Iran, Afghanistan, and Pakistan through Amsterdam to New York. She understood that real money could no longer be made in sugar, cocoa or coffee. It lay in oil, cocaine or women.

At thirteen she'd gone to the man to ask for work. He'd never been charged with shooting her father. Her father had been a big man, her mother said. Maria Estella found it hard to see how he could look like a deer even on the darkest night. By the time Maria Estella went to see him, the man owned a fleet of light airplanes and managed a small island in the Orinoco Delta that specialised in hiding fugitives and processing high-grade cocaine. Soon she was travelling with him, listening, her chameleon-colouring making the men in the rooms doubt her presence in the shadows. She learned to trade and distribute cocaine. She learned to sell the guns that arrived with each shipment, part protection and part cargo. She learned to kill.

But when they kidnapped Maria Estella, Dougla told Chale nothing of this because Micheline, Dougla's woman, had told him nothing of it.

★

When Chale turns up at the beach-house at the end of the second day, Dougla is sitting at the kitchen table reading the papers, eating a plate of stewed chicken and rice. In front of him is another plate of neatly sliced avocado. Chale is hungry but Micheline doesn't offer him food. Chale has been guarding the woman all day, sitting outside the latrine and listening to her shift around inside. They've paid one of the villagers to watch her through the night so he can sleep. The village is not far from here.

Dougla's house leads onto the beach. Just that morning, the villagers had pulled seine in front of the house, the net coming in slowly, spilling the dying fish onto the sand. Most of the villagers know that a woman is being kept in a backyard latrine. She's hidden across the road, up a track past wild guava and fat-pork trees, but it's not far. Dougla supports all the church bazaars and pays for the school's sport supplies. The papers say every village has a Robin Hood and he supposes that's what he is to them. Whenever there's a job, they cook food and lend their latrines.

"Let the woman bathe," Chale tells Dougla when he is leaving. "I'll fill a bucket and take it for her."

He is shame to say he is sorry for the woman, but the place is so damn hot and the latrine so stink, he wouldn't leave a dog there for long. It has been a long day. Good thing this job isn't supposed to last long because he's begun to wonder if he has the stomach for it. To shoot someone and walk away is one thing – you can tell yourself all kind of thing to justify it. But to sit and watch someone suffer, that took real stones. She looked like a nice lady and he's still vexed with himself that he pushed the gun in her mouth. She'd been so frightened when he'd pulled down her pants for her to pee. But he wasn't interested in raping no big woman. When he'd had to help her, he was sad for her, thinking of his mother's panties hanging on the clothesline in their backyard. He wouldn't want his mother in some latrine. He knows his mother is proud of his pretty brown colour and that he has his Bajan granny's eyes, a funny kind of grey that makes big hardback women give him talk when they pass him downtown. His home is nice too. A decent house in Belmont. But people still have it in their head that bandit could only come in one colour, and they have to be poor and downtrodden. It's that kind of mentality that made room for him to climb up. His father works hard as a clerk at Hi Lo Food Stores, but Chale's too smart for that life; he wants to be rich with a pretty wife on his arm and a garage full of fancy cars.

"Wait for me outside," says Dougla between mouthfuls.

Chale has to pass Micheline to leave the room. She doesn't move aside to let him by so he has to press his back against the sideboard and sidle past her. Talk on the town is that she's the real boss, bad like crab, the only girl-child of a rich, high-brown family. Chale has heard her talking to her mother on the phone: Hello, Mumm-ya. Chale is trying to listen to Micheline and Dougla who are talking softly in the other room. He will learn if he keeps his ears open. This is like school and he thinks he is learning from the best. There has been just one phone call.

"Forty-eight hours tops," Dougla is saying. "Her man can cover the ransom. He will pay if he has to."

"I think you should let her go," says Micheline.

Chale cannot see that she has stopped counting the money in the suitcase. He cannot see that she is suddenly very frightened at the possibilities of what they have done.

"Dougla, there's a lot of money here. This is not a small operation."

Dougla sucks his teeth, a long leisurely steupse.

"You think I could make money if I walked away just so? You think that is how I make money, Micheline?"

Chale hears the newspapers give an irritated shuffle.

"It supposed to come tomorrow night; we'll wait it out."

Chale cannot see that Micheline is standing over the suitcase, her hand to her mouth, thinking, thinking, thinking.

Maria Estella needs to pee badly. She's been holding it all night because she's afraid of the man guarding her. In the middle of the night, he came in and peed a long donkey-stream pee in the bucket, right in front of her. She's listening for Chale. She'd heard him say that he'd be back on Monday morning and she'll call him when he comes. Until then, she'll hold it. She may have slept for an hour or two but it can't have been longer than that. She is trying to imagine the man's next move.

By late Monday night, Dougla sends a message to Chale that the ransom has been dropped. Chale is to pick up the retrieval team in a stolen Cortina Ghia with new plates. It is just four young boys he's given some small change. Thirty years on will be a different story. Thirty years on there will be smart phones and GPS tracking. But in the 1980s, on that night, it was all new territory. And somehow they'd pulled it off. When they pulled up at the Valsayn traffic lights, the highway was empty, the backseat of little boys silent.

Chale is the boss that night, but he is nervous about the pickup. The money is supposed to be in the market by the Croisee, the Sunday night market, packed with vendors. No one notices the boys as they spread out among the lettuce and tomatoes, the dasheen and the eddoes. The ransom is packed in a jute sack, the kind used to pack cocoa for market, hidden behind the decapitated head of a slaughtered cow. The ransom sack says **Attention Mr. Ali** in big black letters. The whole operation takes less than six minutes and they are back in the car. The boy counter wears surgical gloves as he checks the money for counterfeit, counting the packets quickly. An hour later they are outside Dougla's beach house, just beyond the periphery of Mafeking village.

Take her to town, carry her on the Lady Young Road, just past the lookout and throw her down the hill. That is the instruction Dougla gives Chale in front of Maria Estella, who stands shivering outside the latrine, a dog chain tied loosely around her ankle.

"Lady Young?" Chale repeats, looking from Dougla to Maria Estella and back again. "Lady Young? Why we don't just drop her close to the man. That was the plan."

Dougla looks at Chale for a long time before spitting on the ground and walking away. Chale cannot know that the instruction has come from Micheline who'd pondered the problem like a math sum all Sunday night. If they let Maria

Estella live, she'd lead the man to them. It had to be Lady Young and it had to be done by Chale.

"Come auntie," Chale clicks his fingers at her as if she's a dog. "Come and bathe."

At first she will not come and she holds stubbornly to the side of the flimsy galvanise structure, cutting her hand on the sharp edges of the metal framework. As he pulls her, she grunts with exertion and he can hear the tightness in her throat. Lady Young. The bodies pile up there, hidden in the long grass and overgrown steps of the carved mountain. They both know what Lady Young means. Dougla has changed the rules on Chale. The woman is pulling hard now, grunting and cursing, but he pries her hands away from the wall and leads her to the makeshift bath.

The threadbare towel smells of mildew and the garish nightie is meant for rosy bedroom light. The word *Sexy* is emblazoned in black on the frilly short skirt.

"Do I have to come in with you?" His voice is kind because she is crying.

When she does not answer, he lets her in, unspooling more of the dog chain that keeps her tied to him.

"Is okay, Auntie. We will talk. Is okay."

Maria Estella strips behind the few planks of wood and galvanized sheeting that make a makeshift bath out of a lone tap. It's been years since she's smelt herself, that funky odour that belongs to her alone. Sometimes she's caught a whiff of it on the man, but now it is concentrated, pungent. Even though she is alone she turns her back to slip her panties off as if the boy can still see and smell her. She squats by the tap and scrubs with a bar of green Palmolive soap that has a crown cork stuck in the bottom to stop it from sticking to the concrete. The bottom of the soap is slimy and leaves long trails of green scum on her fingers when she puts it back on the mildewed concrete plinth under the tap.

★

The house where Maria Estella lived with her mother had two bedrooms. A tiny kitchen looked out over the road and the small living room was lined with raw planks of pine that bled tiny beads of oil from its knots. Her mother grew begonias and ferns on the front balcony and each morning she squatted over a bucket and peed her morning stream before diluting it with water and dousing the plants. When her mother was pregnant the begonias grew wide fat silver leaves and the baby's-breath ferns jumped their pots to catch in the damp soil under the stairs.

Maria Estella slept with the twin girls in the back bedroom that bunched up between the mountain and the cannonball tree that sent long branches through the window over the sleeping girls. Maria Estella slept between the toddlers, their little bodies following the lines of her body. The tree grew round red and yellow flowers off its bark – wide impossible things with frilly edges. High in the trees' canopy, mosquito larvae bred in spiky bromeliad nurseries, which released them, fully winged and hungry, into the bedrooms of the small house.

Maria Estella remembered how she and her mother chewed green pawpaw and kissed the pulp into the mouths of the toddlers. They brought buckets of cold river water to the house, bathing and sapping infant skin so hot that she could remember the drops evaporating. The littlest one held out her arms to Maria Estella, mewling and reaching up, her tiny fists opening and closing. Water. Water. Two days later the doctor arrived wheezing from his climb up the hill, his car hissing gently on the road below. Dengue, he said. Empty your barrels and turn over

54

your buckets. Cut your trees. There is an epidemic in town. It seemed that this was all he could say over the tiny, lifeless bodies, gently laid head to toe like dolls. Her mother wanted to bury them where they could see them and talk to them. The village priest buried them in the Catholic cemetery that lay on the edge of the cliff. Everyone knew that, sooner or later, the unanchored bones would slip into the ocean.

After this, Maria Estella slept in her mother's bed, windows open to the night breezes. In the other room, her mother lay naked on the floor, her arms and legs spread on a black sheet, the mosquitoes hovering, grey and gauzy.

The villagers said Maria Estella showed signs of the pawpaw cure when her skin grew mossy and tender, beautiful and verdant. Her mother lay in the other room until her skin turned ochre and cold. When the village policeman and the doctor came, the policeman remembered the night her father had been dropped by a single bullet. It was he who gave her the man's number. Call him, he said, his voice, flutish and high, and tell him your mother is dead and your father was not a deer.

★

"When you finish, throw the clothes out and put on the ones I gave you."

The boy's voice is hushed and she realises they are moving her without the village knowing. The night air is cold and her teeth chatter as she dries with the damp towel. The boy slips a pillowcase over her head. The boy is still gentle, no shoving and pushing. They walk for a long time before coming out into a clearing where the small sedan sits dwarfed by the forest trees. There is no one to hold Maria Estella down in the back seat and it is here on this lonely back road on the edge of the forest that they must begin their compromise, each bargaining for their life.

When the sedan drives off, Maria Estella is in the front seat next to Chale. He is bareback and she wears his shirt over the nighty, still shivering.

★

"Are you absolutely sure you can trust him?" Micheline asks.

"One hundred percent," Dougla says. "That boy love me like a father. The man will kill him before he has a chance to make it off that Lady Young road."

"So we good, Dougla? You sure?"

"We real good. Better than good."

"We'll lie low for a while. Hide the money in the forest."

★

By time he's made it back into town with Maria Estella sitting bold-faced in the front seat of the stolen Cortina, Chale knows he doesn't have what it takes to be a professional kidnapper. He'll have to tap some other lucrative stream. There are little tributaries breaking away from the river of enterprise that followed the wave of cocaine in the 80s. The possibilities are endless for a young boy with ambition.

She tells him on the back road in Guayaguayare who paid the ransom. The name that comes out of her mouth makes his stomach drop. If this was the man who'd paid the ransom, that makes Maria Estella the man's woman. The Spanish woman. Even he has heard of the Spanish woman. Does Dougla know? His tongue sticks to the roof of his mouth.

"Was there a woman?" she asks.

"Only Micheline."

"Micheline?" Maria Estella now knows who is behind it

56

all. Micheline. Micheline. She'd been the man's woman before her.

Chale avoids the Lady Young road on the way back into town, coming, instead, down the Beetham highway, past the shanties on the right, the landfill on the left, all the garbage and rubbish from the island heaped in stinking piles for the corbeaux to plunder and loot. All the while Maria Estella sits planning, her green skin pulsing, the plan unfolding in her mind like the unpacking of nesting boxes.

Chale doesn't hear what she says to the man when he smuggles her into his parents' home after three a.m. and directs her to the telephone in the kitchen. He wonders if she can smell his mother's breath on the phone because he knows his mother will have been on the phone all night calling every one of his friends. Chale had told his parents he was going to Mayaro for a week with friends, but he'd expected to be back by last night. He knows his mother will be worried.

Even though it is three in the morning, Belmont is still playing Road March 1985, "Soucouyant" by Crazy, unfurling through the fretwork jalousies and from under doors, even though it is already Lent.

"Hide me for three days," she says, whispering as she comes out into black night to find him. "That's what he says to do. Can you do that?"

It is difficult to read her face in the night but he imagines the soft ochre freckles forming along the bridge of her nose, spreading in a mask, while she thinks. As if she has known all along that this is how it would end up.

"Will my family be safe?"

"Yes, I can promise you that. He knows you were played by them."

She hides in the outside room at his parent's Belmont

home, the one his grandmother lived in before she died. She eats smuggled food from his mother's pot for three days, raising her head from the pillow on the small cot in the backroom to take small bites of choice pieces that Chale has handpicked from the pot. He brings titbits of tannia and plantain fritters, tender pieces of stewed chicken with white rice, soft macaroni pie, tempting her as if she were a difficult child. And all along he apologises. I'm sorry, he says. I'm sorry. Tell me what to do.

★

Thirty years on, the mountains still grow their emerald pelts for the rain. Chale is proud of the quiet hum of his Porsche Cayenne when he turns into a quiet street in Woodbrook. The house is one of the last of its kind on the street – the kind of house he'd been raised to think was his ambition. With their delicate fretwork, it seemed as if the ground itself had grown these houses out of the Taino bones-mangrove sludge that made everything in the ground bloom obscenely. Maria Estella would be happy to see him. It has been months since his last visit.

"Maria Estella? Maria Estellaaa?" With his shouting, the pack of pot hounds start barking in the back.

"Chale? Is that you?" She comes to the door wearing an old print housedress. She is wiping her face with a towel and pulling a brush through her hair, walking forward to unlatch the gate. In the time since he's last seen her, she's aged that bit more. Not anything that you can put your finger on, just a subtle desiccation of the body – the marrow calling the flesh home. She puts her cheek forward to be kissed. The skin under his lips is warm and soft with the lightest of amber fuzz running along her jawline.

"Come, Chale. It's been too long. Come and tell me." She is already walking back into the drawing room with its familiar floral-printed Morris chairs. Above the door leading into the kitchen is a new statue of the Sacred Heart of Jesus, the heart overgrown and blowsy, disturbing and garish. Has she gone religious? He's never seen any sign of it before. Maybe once. All those years ago when they'd first met. He'd heard her pray that night.

"How your tomatoes going, boy?" She comes out through the door with a glass of lime juice covered with a small-netted doily, its gay beads holding the thin net on the surface of the glass. She's gone to the trouble of adding a dash of angostura bitters, the darker, heavier liquid swirling through the lighter coloured juice. Always been a good hostess. He listens for Micheline's voice. There'd been a kidnapping that morning and with the sun just going down, people will be getting into position to work through the night. That's how it works now. Tonight, the operation will be all over the city. While they sleep, the negotiators will be up with the family and the Anti-Kidnapping Squad. Impossible to imagine they'd been able to do anything at all in 1985. Thirty years on no decent kidnapping occurs without a counter and a driver, one on the phone to the boss, constantly changing SIM cards to foil the trace and the last man there as the runner to pick up the package. They are always young and smart. Chale recently heard that a team used a boy from the International School. Another one was supposed to be a contender for an island scholarship at CIC. Those priests would spin if they knew what these Catholic schoolboys were getting up to on a Sunday night in 2015.

Micheline is one of the best negotiators on the island, working out of a back room in Maria Estella's house. In the early days, before there were professional negotiators hashing it out like overpriced lawyers, Micheline had dealt with the families directly, her convent accent creating a trust that persuaded the families to part with their money easily. Now it is different; now she deals with the negotiator from the Anti-Kidnapping-Squad and he is never swayed by her uppity accent. But still Maria Estella keeps her, under the weight of a key, in the back room.

"So tell me, how those tomatoes going?"

★

In times of heavy rain, the Orinoco Delta floods and any number of things can make their way on floating clumps of water hyacinths with their gay violet flowers. The water turns brackish and sweet, brown streaks filtering out and turning the water a deep muddy green. On that moonlit night so long ago, someone had made a smart hat, a type of bowler hat not often seen in these islands, papering it with counterfeit money. Dougla had come out to return the ransom money. The man had sent a message to meet near Quinam, but by the time Chale and Maria Estella arrived there was no sign of him or Dougla.

"How do you know he'll come?" Chale had asked Maria Estella on the long drive out.

"He will come," she'd said. "He wants to live and he thinks it is as easy as returning money."

As he'd walked towards the beach, Chale had seen the hat at the tideline. From where they stood it looked as if it dressed a rogue coconut – perhaps a swanky coconut, picked for its bravado from all the other coconuts on the tree. The ransom money was still in its jute bag, under a pile of copra and discarded coconut shells. Maria Estella sat on a beached log on the silver beach and began counting.

"Bury the head," she said, counting, her mouth silently sounding the numbers.

Chale had looked back at her, sick to his stomach.

"Bury it deep behind the trees so the dogs can't get it."

60

He'd had to go back to the car to get a shovel; it took him over an hour to bury the head, hat and all. They never spoke of it again, but after that everyone knew he belonged to the Spanish woman, knew that his loyalty was only to her. She'd taught him everything he knew. Things might have turned out differently if Micheline had offered him a plate of food that night.

For many months, Chale dreamed of Dougla, his mind working hard to attach Dougla's head to his body. When a body was buried without a head, would it return to look for it? He'd heard his mother say her own mother had come back to look for shoes, enraged that her only daughter had buried her with bare feet. Would that also apply to a head? But for the rest of his life, when he dreamed Dougla back, the stocky, bulky body would be instantly familiar, the jolt of fear only coming from the confused, disembodied head that opened and closed its mouth like a fish out of water.

It would be years before he met Maria Estella's man, deep in the Orinoco Delta. But the man had let him live and Chale had been put on the payroll, his loyalty to Maria Estella never questioned. Chale had picked up Micheline in a grocery not long after. They'd come upon each other so quickly that the air was suddenly turbulent. They hurried past the bottles of ketchup and the jars of salsa, Micheline carrying her new self like a fragile package, Chale pushing her quietly into the car, the gun a mere formality.

★

Sometimes Micheline writes poetry when she is bored. She slips these under the door for Maria Estella and asks her to keep them safe. They are two old ladies now. What harm could come of it?

The lilies in the pond drown like loons
Outstretched white necks
Drinking rain on water stippled as a moon
Stretched thin as any Saturday

Maria Estella keeps them all in a binder.

"Who knows?" she tells Chale. "We may have a real poet on our hands. Everyone has a different side."

CENTIPEDE

When Marcella approaches, Poodle is drawing charts on a makeshift blackboard at the back of the house. He's made the board from a piece of pitch-pine painted flat black. At night, Poodle and the other estate workers draw a dartboard on it with red and white chalk. Each morning they wipe it clean before they start their day. Henri, Marcella's husband says he doesn't mind the darts. It's the gambling that can get out of hand. This morning, Poodle is waiting to start the lesson. Marcella has brought him a cup of coffee and he blows on it while he waits for her to pull her copybook out of her bag. This morning he is dressed in old jeans, a white merino, and sturdy boots. Always slim, his jeans are held up by one of Henri's old belts.

"You watching?" His hand holding the chalk is hovering in front of the board.

First mark – Centipede

Next to him, her skin is pale. When her hair's wet, Poodle tells her it shimmers like kerosene on a hot day. It's that kind of brown. Poodle is the colour of a tonka bean, brown with a hint of red. At the tops of his cheekbones, the skin is shiny as if polished. Marcella has never told Marie Adele, her husband's mother, she's related to Poodle. Henri knows they are something like fourth cousins. You can't really consider that family.

Poodle writes in painstaking detail, listing all the things

that might cause a person to play Play Whe's mark 1 –
Centipede: cutlass, penknife, small gun, key, pen, candle,
stick, smoking, chain, cigarettes, lights, bar, glass, women,
snakes, scissors, tailor, razor, barber, head, old people, old
anyhow, back-to-front, upside-down, wrong-side.

"Centipede. So if you dream an old lady hold you down
and cut off all your hair, what you think you will play? What
mark you think will play that day?" Poodle stops, his head
cocked. "If you were a betting kind of woman?"

She doesn't have to think. "Mark one. Centipede."

"Right. You getting it. And if you really into it, a dream
like that is gold. Think about it. This thing is a science. Write
down the signs."

She makes notes in a small pale-blue copybook with the
crest of the village school on the front and rows of timeta-
bles at the back. Poodle is explaining why she needs to make
the move to the illegal whe whe. She's too talented to waste
her time playing for the lottery board. Play Whe is safe but
whe whe will make her rich. Talent isn't just about reading
dreams. It's understanding that a mark can be a secret,
hidden thing. It's knowing what number to pick and understanding why that number must win.

"You want to draw it? Look, I have a picture here." He
pulls a creased poster out the pocket of his jeans and hands
it to her. She begins to copy the fat Chinaman whose body
is carved up like a suckling pig. Thirty-six pieces of
Chinapoo. From his head to his toe, every part of his body
is something to gamble on. Poodle has brought her a
newly cracked cocoa pod knowing she loves the white
pulp that coats the lavender seeds. She rolls a bean in her
mouth while she draws, her teeth gently scraping the
surface. She knows even the smallest nick in the
unfermented bean releases a black bitterness. Delicious-

ness is only born sweating under banana leaves, fermenting flavour into the bean.

A natural, Poodle calls her. She likes the way he looks at her. The way he rocks back on the old wooden chair in the back room and looks at her under lidded eyes. Poodle isn't that closely related to her. She'd sat and worked it out on a piece of paper a long time ago. It wasn't as if he was a first cousin.

"You will teach me how to play it? The illegal one?" She's still drawing in her copybook, carefully colouring the different parts of Chinapoo.

"I have to teach you. It's my moral obligation." He smiles, teeth lining his mouth with authority. "No one ever tell you about Ho Leung? Your mother's family? How he walk off the boat with not a word of English in his mouth and set up a top class whe whe operation right here in the valley?" When she said no, his steupse told her all she needed to know about his irritation with her parents' hurry to shed their past and marry their girls off to white creoles like her husband Henri.

"Ho Leung was my great-grandfather. Man make a frigging fortune, yes." Poodle is rolling a joint, licking the tip of his finger and picking out seeds and twigs. "Your blood in the mix too. I feel you inherit something there. Some blood pass down."

Marcella imagines the gift of symbols twirling down ancient Chinese blood. Choosing her, no one else. Not even Poodle, who has moved in because Henri bought a cocoa farm six months ago. Four acres larger than your father's own, Henri had said, visibly puffing. All his savings – all of her savings – gone to buy twenty acres of abandoned cocoa farm, a derelict cocoa house, some broken down farm equipment, and a pretty fretwork house with nasty plumbing. There is even a pasture sloping down in front of the house where Henri tells Marcella she can keep a horse.

In spite of all the sacrifices, in spite of her law degree, she's been delivered right back to her parents in the valley; she's been delivered back to Poodle. The idea of Marcella being delivered back to them amuses Poodle and he tells her it makes her husband a large freckled stork. Once that image is planted in her head it is hard to remove. Henri is a looker. Tall and lanky with beautifully hinged joints and long slender feet, his wedding ring sits with grace on his hand. After nearly six months on the farm, his hands are still beautiful and graceful.

She draws with concentration, shading in the lines that divide the Chinaman. It is almost finished with its careful notes and arrows.

"Tell me more about the banker, Ho Leung." She wipes the sticky pulp off her hands.

Poodle leans back and lights his joint. "Someone had to be the banker, you understand? His turf was right here by the river. Said he could read the signs and understand the dream symbols better when he was close to the water. In those days, it was a purist kind of thing. Didn't have Trini marks like jammet back then. Chinee man must have a different word for that kind of woman."

The word jammet hangs in the air. Jammet. A loose woman. A woman who sleeps with men other than her husband. The word catches Marcella's breath.

"Each day the banker call a mark. Decides the number that will be the mark of the day. And everyone waiting to hear what mark will call, what mark the banker will buss that day. Any number from one to thirty-six. Every number meaning something different. Once the mark buss, a set of runners take off around the village and collect the bets.

66

Everybody dropping their bets at a different place. Some betting one dollar, some betting one hundred, the number and the bet on a little piece of paper. When all the bets collect, the banker pays himself and then pays out."

"That's it?" She is pleased with her drawing. "That doesn't seem hard. I could be a banker." She knows people imagine that when they lie down and dream it means something. Who wants to believe a lottery board can climb into your head and call a mark?

"Well yes, Miss Big-shot-now-start-to-play-want-to-be banker!" Poodle hunches forward, the cords in his shoulders moving, laughter making him cough. "First lady banker. You want to kill your husband? He will dead with shame."

"Why I have to tell him anything? If I pay you? You teaching me already."

Poodle brings the joint to his mouth, inhaling deeply and holding his breath until it seeps in thin blue lines from his nostrils. Then he pinches it out and hides it in his matchbox. He wipes the board clean, done with her for now, the red smudging under his cloth before it disappears.

"Wait, Poodle. You will place the last bet tonight? The whole thing on one mark."

"Oh Jesus, Marcella. Look at the time; you will get my ass fired. Yes, I'll put everything on the last mark tonight." He walks to the edge of the paved area to look up at the sky. "Henri will be looking for me. Rain nearly here and we have plenty cocoa in the sun." With his cutlass hanging safely in the leather case that he has braided onto Henri's belt, he disappears down the path towards the cocoa house. Marcella stays a few minutes longer, reading her notes before turning to the front of her copybook where she has carefully written out a recipe for quiche Lorraine.

He's right. They have a lot of cocoa in the sun. Poodle's room is next to the kitchen, which is outside the main house. She started sleeping with Poodle out of spite really. Plain and simple. Marcella entertaining herself, negotiating her spite in the same way she'd once negotiated marine leases for ocean floor – before her husband asked her to give up her job and help him run a cocoa farm. Every time she leaves her sleeping husband for Poodle, spite fortifies her. What are the odds of Henri giving up his idea of the land, the odds of eliminating the tiny vendettas in her head? She balances these odds against the odds of getting caught sleeping with Poodle. The nights she feels a mark coming, she leaves her sleeping husband to climb into Poodle's bed, as voracious as she'd been as a teenager. Afterwards, she stumbles back to her room where she dreams deep green dreams. She dreams clearly and lucidly, waking fresh and smooth in the morning, ready to play her mark. A small duffel bag hides the money Poodle brings back after each win, his tonka-bean skin flushed with excitement.

The sex had been like that with Henri in the beginning. They'd met in a bar on the Avenue. She'd never had a boyfriend and suddenly there was Henri. Two lawyers casually introduced on Friday night after work. So complementary, their friends said; you two would have beautiful children. Marcella's turmeric eyes luminescent against her coffee skin, Henri a freckled-skin creole with pale blue eyes and a bloodline going back to the 1700s. Their intoxication fed on submerged desires. For Marcella, Henri offered a life of respectability and comfort, a climb up in the world. For Henri, Marcella was the land, a chance to return to the cocoa of his ancestors – a mutual misalignment of intoxication.

The French creole estates had been lost to the English bankers. This was at the heart of Henri's land lust. Marie Adele's grandfather was the King of Cocoa. It was said he'd been so powerful, he had a direct line to God. It was a standard joke even Marcella knew. The La Roulettes only spoke to the De Marquises and the De Marquises only spoke to God. But in the end, after witches broom decimated the cocoa, the English bankers and Scottish overseers had taken the estates. This was the injustice Henri sought to redress whatever the cost to his new marriage.

Just two years in, just when they'd been starting to think about having a baby, he'd decided to buy the farm. When he borrowed from the bank and his mother, she'd realised he was serious. "I'm not going back. I'm not," she'd told him. "Why should I give up my career?" But in the end, what could she do? He was her husband and she was not ready to let go of the marriage. So she'd given in. He'd needed her savings as well. Think, he said, think of the money made when cocoa was king. Millions of dollars. Think of the life the planters enjoyed. That time will come again. Think, Marcella wanted to say to him. You want me to think? *You* think. Think of why your mother never invites my parents to dinner. Think of why she has never introduced her friends to me. Think of why she suddenly had flu on our wedding day. Think of why it matters that I am the daughter of a cocoa farmer, not an aristocratic French creole planter. Instead, Marcella says, over and over, that Henri knows nothing.

Henri's family would have looked out over the indentured Indians, Chinese, Portuguese, mainland Venezuelans and newly emancipated blacks, watching them marry and mix until whole villages took on the polished cheekbones of their region. Their friends in Port of Spain tell her how lovely it must be to go back to the land. So honest, they say – this while she looks at their pedicured feet – the life she'd thought she was getting.

Making money from cocoa is hard work, but Henri says cocoa is the next black gold. Don't think of it as a loan, he'd told his mother when he'd asked for the first money. Think of it as an investment. When the oil runs out, we will be ahead of the next boom. He's after the couverture chocolate market, the ones that look for more cocoa butter in the raw lumps of cocoa ground from the beans. There is money to be made if you have a vision. He talks a good talk at parties. Don't they know that all the fancy chocolatiers in France have their chocolate makers buy directly from the Trinidad farms now?

Watch he doesn't keep a mistress in town and have you out here picking cocoa. French creoles are different to us, Marcella's mother whispered when they moved back to the valley.

Today Marie Adele is coming to tea and Henri will ask her if they can borrow more money. Marcella will place all the money she has in her duffle bag on one mark. This way she hopes to make enough to pay back both Marie Adele and the bank. The farm will then be in her name. She never doubts that she will win with this mark. She has won with every other one that she has played. The marks swim up from sleep or they cross her in the house like ghosts. Today, the mark is all about Marie Adele. It will emanate off her, that much Marcella knows. So she must make Marie Adele comfortable in her home. Make her relaxed and happy to be there. Marie Adele has not visited them very often since the move; today will be only be the second time she's driven out to see them and Marcella wonders if she suspects she's being summoned for money.

In the kitchen she begins assembling flour, butter, water, and ice water for the quiche Lorraine.

"Rain is coming!" she calls out the window, as if Poodle has not said the very same thing to her ten minutes before. "The cocoa… cover the cocoa." These small duplicitous gestures add layers of guilt. As if the act of calling out of the window will signal to Henri that she's been in the kitchen all morning preparing for his mother.

As she pinches the dough she imagines that she has Marie Adele's pale fingers; long, dry and cool. She has already cut the butter into the flour and is trying to think calm thoughts to keep her fingertips cold. But in the small kitchen, humidity coats everything with a damp film and causes her hair to stick to the back of her neck. She dips her fingers into the water bowl. She'd never heard of quiche before she met Henri. Her mother baked sturdy pies with tough crusts, the kind that could hold a whole pot of guava stew and not buckle under the weight of the fruit. These were pies that did not melt in your mouth but had to be cut firmly and chewed with a concentration that brought its own pleasure. She kneads the pastry gently but it falls apart, refusing to come together even though she adds little drops of the freezing water. The water is icy, the little silver chips melting around her hot fingers. She begins to handle the pastry mixture gently. She keeps her hands light and soft, imagining a tender, flaky crust as she rubs the butter into a grainy mix. So much trouble for a pie. So much trouble for a quiche Lorraine.

As she works in this battered estate house kitchen, she dimly senses something of the dip and sway rhythm of her childhood, the deeply satisfying hum that ran below the surface of the most mundane of chores. The outline of the mark is already there, misty on its way to the surface of her mind. As a child she'd danced the cocoa with her sisters, the three of them shuffling and moving through the beans, sloughing off the last of the fleshy pulp and exposing the beans with their undertones of mauve, lavender and grey. Sometimes the small transistor radio was brought out onto the porch, all three swaying and dipping to the tinny sound of the latest calypso.

Poodle and Henri are on the drying rack, pulling the casters to slide the low roof over the beans. Behind them, Marcella can see the rain coming down the valley in waves, the sound thundering ahead of the first heavy drops. The immortelle flowers glow red against the Santa Cruz mountains and the cocoa trees bend their leaves. On the hill near the house, the bois canot leaves are turning in the wind, showing their silver undersides before falling. The men pull the roof closed and take shelter under the cocoa house. They stand together, Henri blowing his cigarette smoke out into the rain, the mist and smoke clouding their faces. Even though he wears the same high Wellington boots as them all, Henri's boots look like a costume, his stride exaggerated and clumsy. She notices Henri worrying something with his toe. With his hand braced against the walls of the shed, Henri pushes his foot deep into the pile of dried cocoa husks and clears a space with his foot. Poodle hands him a rake and together they rake back the black husks to expose something. It must be a snake, or a scorpion, or even a nest of tiny, pale brown scorpions or any kind of awful thing that likes to hide beneath the rotting layer of discarded husks.

"Henri!" HENRI!" She is out the door and running, her heart pounding. She doesn't stop to notice that they are not alarmed. She only thinks of the dangers that lie unseen. On the bottom shelf of the fridge lie the vials of anti-snake venin with the Ministry of Health stamp. Last week she recorded each expiry date on the calendar. Technically a doctor should administer the anti-venin, but old Dr. Chin has taught them all how to do it. As angry as she is with Henri, she is terrified that something will happen to him. The idea of his death frightens her deeply and because of this, she thinks she must still love him.

Under the shed, she sees what they have uncovered. A mother cat with a litter of ginger kittens, the little mouths mewling and tiny. Around them the rain has slowed to a shimmer of air, condensation evaporating like a mirage on the hot driveway.

"Look, Marcella." Henri is gentle as he squats and pats the mother cat's triangular head. Below his hand, the cat purrs and rubs the side of her face into his palm. "Kittens."

The farm has splintered something deep in their young marriage. It has uncovered, in both of them, an intractable core of self, a point from which neither will budge. She can't blame him entirely because she married him for love, yes, but also for a sense of security and access to a world that has been closed to her. Looking at the beauty of the land, it is hard to believe neat rows of cocoa trees have the power to burn out a marriage. But the marriage is smouldering on. Marcella picks up the cat and her kittens and takes them into the kitchen with her. There she assembles a makeshift bed out of a cardboard box and lines it with old towels. As a child, her mother's kitchen always had young animals. Small chicks brought indoors at night, puppies around your feet. The cat settles, an orange comma around her blind young.

Marcella keeps the duffle bag hidden in the spare room, the one that stores all the remnants of their Port of Spain life. A bicycle, a menu for the sushi place on the Avenue, marriage presents of china and Waterford crystal yet to be unpacked and incongruous on the estate. She has tried to make the room cheerful and it is a sweet room with its broderie anglaise curtains and chenille bedspread. From this room, the northern range is blue, the filter of the savonetta tree making it look aquatic. After she has assembled the quiche and prepared it for baking, Marcella lies down here and closes her eyes. She has not decided whether she will stay after she wins. The dim light pulls her under into a light sleep where she dreams of misshapen pies and missed deadlines. When she wakes she can tell by the angle of the sun that it is past three.

Dry mouthed and groggy, she heads for the kitchen. There is no sign of Henri. The kitchen is the best room in the morning but now the western sun is merciless. She should have cooled the pastry dough, but the fridge is packed with produce that Poodle delivers to Port of Spain every Friday. One shelf is full of eggs, another full of mango anchar, fresh coconut chutney, tightly packed parcels of chadon beni, ziplock bags of fresh cocoa, the pulp still clinging to the pods.

The quiche in the oven is timed to emerge at 3.30. Through the layers of heat and the misted glass of the oven door, Marcella can see the quiche growing into a monstrous thing. She's ignored the instructions to bake the pastry blind and it bubbles and rises with a determination that surprises her. But when it emerges, it is perfect. Crisp around the edges, the deep yellow of farm yolks and the rich marbling of bacon just visible below the surface. Henri is suddenly behind her, his hair neatly combed, his face fresh. They have both made an effort.

"You've made a better quiche than Marie Adele." He

smiles at her and she smiles back. At times like this she doesn't think of Poodle.

When Marie Adele comes through the door, Marcella is grating raw cocoa into a pot of milk. To this she adds a dash of cinnamon, some clove, and a tap of butter. Finally she adds sugar. Marcella is bathed and fresh, her kerosene hair braided down her back. She wears a white cotton shirt with small wooden buttons and a pair of white shorts. She has chosen her shoes carefully, picking out a simple pair of Grecian-style sandals.

They sit on the small patch of grass in front of the house surrounded by torch and ginger lilies, balisiers and crotons. They eat small wedges of quiche on cloth napkins and drink Marcella's cocoa. Marie Adele has brought a bottle of wine. They do not speak of money. Instead they speak of the weather and the kittens in the house. They sit into the twilight until Henri gets up to turn on lights and bring out the citronella candles.

The evening is lavender lit, the mountains a blue wound on the sky, when Marie Adele rises with a wail. A centipede balances on the back of her skirt, swaying gently, one hundred legs projecting off the hard shiny carapace. Already it is easy to imagine her calf red and inflamed. She wails more loudly still, pain making her voice shrill and high. To look over her shoulder she must twist her neck unnaturally. The centipede must have hidden under the wrought-iron garden chair. Henri stamps hard on the fallen insect, the brittle exoskeleton losing its sheen before their eyes.

Now is when the banker would choose the mark. Think Marcella. THINK. Tell a narrative based on the mark and its spirit partner. Centipede partners with dead person and the spirit match is dead man. She takes Marie Adele inside, trying to remember her notes. In the blue light of the bathroom, Marie Adele white calf is purpling and swelling. Marcella wrings a cold cloth and wipes the older woman's face gently, forming a triangle of the corner and gently wiping her tears and smoothing her cheeks with the cool cloth. Marie Adele's face is flushed with hot red areas under her eyes and around her nostrils and she cries harder when Marcella makes her swallow an antihistamine and wraps the leg in a cold compress. No one dies from the sting of a centipede, but no doubt, there will be fever and pain.

Marcella smooths Marie Adele's hair away from her face, stroking her cheeks like a child's and making comforting noises deep in her throat.

"Come," she says to Marie Adele, "you can sleep here tonight."

In the hallway, Marie Adele holds onto Marcella and cries hiccupping tears like a child and Marcella understands that Marie Adele is no longer crying over a centipede sting. Together they phone Marie Adele's helper and let her know that Marie Adele will spend the night with Marcella and Henri. Then they phone Marcella's mother who says, yes, yes, of course, I will come. I'm leaving now.

In the kitchen, Henri is on the phone to Dr. Chin. "She can take an antihistamine even though she is on heart medication? You're sure?"

With Henri in the kitchen and Marie Adele resting with a cool cloth on her head, Marcella calls Poodle on his cell phone. She goes into the broderie anglaise room and hands the duffle bag to Poodle through the open Demerara window. Play Number Two. No, I'm sure. I'm positive. Do not play Centipede. Once the bag is gone, Marcella changes the sheets and pulls out the extra blankets from the cupboard. She plumps up the two pillows and turns off the overhead light so that the bedside lamp fills the room with a warm intimate glow. She hangs a spare towel over the back of the chair for Marie Adele and clears two shelves in the cupboard. Marie Adele will sleep here tonight and she wants her to be comfortable in the pretty little room. Outside the window, swung high in the savonetta tree, the pink flowers of the night-blooming cereus are beginning to open, petal by petal.

> Mark 2 – Old lady: woman & child, nurses, women children, dogs, biggest fire, lights.
> Mark 24 – The Queen: eating food, vegetables, fruits, picking fruits, rotten fruit, old, sickness, crying, old people, quarrelling, jammet, women, silver money.

The mark had swum up as cool and clean as a new baby. Later than night, Marcella gives Marie Adele cup after cup of soursop tea to help her sleep and holds her hand. Just to be sure she double-checks her copybook notes. Number 2 – Old Woman partners with 24, the Queen. The corresponding body part, right calf. You can spin so many stories from just three parts. All evening the marks unfold. Secrets hidden like coughs in a handkerchief.

THE WHALE HOUSE

These offshore islands rise out of the water, rugged and black with deep crevices and craggy promontories. Her father used to tell the story of building the house. Dynamite under the water to blow a hole in the hill, a false plateau appearing like a shelf, the hill buckled up behind it. Sometimes, after heavy rain, stones clatter lightly on the roof as the soil shifts and moves behind the house. Her parents' ashes are buried here in the rocky, flinty soil, but Laura and Mark scatter the baby's ashes in the ocean, looking for black-finned porpoises as the talcum-powder dust hovers on the misty spray. When Mark releases the last of the ashes they drive the boat towards the house in silence. Laura is the first to slip over the side, wading carefully towards the shore, eyes on the horizon. Over the years she's learned to watch for scorpion fish and the low-lying stingrays that rise like illusions when dusk slides into the bay.

Mark had cried in the hospital, but now, after they've scattered the ashes, there's just the heat of blame rising off him. Even in the boat, he'd passed her with averted eyes. Later that night, she waits for him lying on her side of the two single beds pushed together. But by the time he comes up from the jetty she is already dreaming hard. Under the sepia mosquito net, she lies on her side, a small feather pillow between her legs. The mosquitoes settle in dark clumps on the netting, whining softly into the night air.

By morning the dreams are gone, flying through the tiny holes in the net in sudden starling movements. The twin beds are pushed together and the net strains to cover both beds. She wakes with the mist of the dreams still heavy in the room and moves up behind her husband, trying to wrap her body around his larger one. To reach him she must lie on the join in the bed. The hard, knotted bump where the mattresses meet bites into her hip, but she lies still, matching her breathing to his soft exhalations; when she feels his breathing change, she knows he's awake. Overnight their legs have tangled, their limbs sealing in the humidity but slowly he inches his leg away with the soft mollusc sound of flesh separating. She rolls back over onto her side and he leaves the room without speaking.

Would the baby have survived if she'd rested in the afternoons, stayed in bed as the doctor had advised? Mark has not accused her of endangering the baby. Such a bald statement would take them to a dangerous edge. So instead it is hovering between them, nebulous and monstrous. She had not rested enough, she knows, but it had been a time of neither wanting nor not wanting, a strangely remote period. It is that indifference that she is exploring, testing it as gently as a tongue on a wound. She'd thought the feeling hidden, so solidly concealed that she'd doubted its potency. But now there is no baby, the grief has come upon her, making her bones hollow.

Outside the window, the tide is changing, the sea frothing and roiling into the tight channel. But beyond, in the harbour, it expands in relieved swells, glad to be past the slick mountain walls. Four months ago, Laura had gone to see Dr. Harnaysingh. She'd made the appointment because at forty-six, her body was suddenly an unknown entity. Once calm and predictable, a source of surety and absolutes, it was now dense, fleshy, prone to thickened skin and odd middle-aged lust. She'd missed three periods, but pregnancy was not something she'd considered. She'd been researching menopause and hormone-replacement options. When she'd told Mark, he'd lifted her nightie, rested his dark head between her ribs and hipbones, and traced gentle circles around the hard space above her pubic bone. She'd imagined a light swooping and fluttering deep inside of her as Mark murmured to the quicksilver heartbeat, that mere conspiracy of cells. A baby.

The day she'd felt the baby's first movements, she cracked three eggs. She separated the yolks from the whites, each yellow globe quivering gently on the edge of a shell as the clear albumin streamed into the bowl. Alone, in their blue bowl, the yolks leaned into one another, separated by the thinnest of membranes. Gently she skewered them, holding the bowl tightly to gain purchase on the slippery surfaces.

When she next saw Dr. Harnaysingh, she lied, smoothly and easily, assuring him that she was being careful and staying off her feet. At home, she continued to bake – cakes, casseroles, soufflés – balancing on the stepladder as she lugged down heavy iron pots and ancient mixing bowls. She even weeded the back stairs, squatting heavily on the mossy concrete, the varicose veins in her ankles thudding in protest.

"Shouldn't you be resting more?" Mark asked.

The baby was born at just twenty eight weeks.

"Come baby, breathe." Dr. Harnaysingh said.

Mark sat in the corner of the room his head in his hands. Laura stretched the lavender baby along the inside of her arms, the perfect feet pressing against her breasts, the heels of her hands supporting the fragile head. Cupping the tender skull with both hands, she kissed the violet fingers, ears and toes, running her fingers along the butterfly eyebrows. To keep her warm she pulled the baby close to her breast, swaddling and rocking her. After three hours, Dr. Harnaysingh sedated her so they could pry the baby from her.

"Can babies feel regret?" Laura asked Dr. Harnaysingh as the opiate dripped into her veins.

Now the ashes have sunk to the bottom of the sea, Mark is downstairs; the musical sound of his spoon beating the cup. The room Laura lies in faces the sea. It was her parents' room. Her father built four rooms, three that face the sea and a smaller one that looks into the flinty soil of the hill. The small room is the nursery with its tiny cots and miniature bunks. When the children were little, she often woke in the night panicked that the toddlers had been swept away in the night currents. A neighbour deeper in the bay had lost a two-year-old that way, the child climbing out of his crib and making his way down the stairs and over the jetty. In those days, Laura's stairs had two wrought iron gates, one at the top and one at the bottom, each padlocked with a little gold key.

From the window she sees Jeannine on the jetty. It still surprises her that this is her firstborn. There is an old photograph of Laura holding Jeannine and smiling at the camera. The caption reads: *What a great big sister! Monos 1982*. She's sure her parents suspected she was sleeping with Mark, but what could they do? It had only stopped when they'd been caught. But by that time she was already pregnant. A small copse of trees runs down the hill stopping before the jetty. Does her mother's plot with medicinal herbs still exist? If her mother were alive, she would know what poultices to place on Laura's aching breasts. She'd had one for a cough and one to lower blood pressure. But Laura only remembers the one meant to flush a womb and make the blood run red and clean. Its romantic name conjured crystal lights and grown-up parties that made you forget the spiky vicious head and bitter green stems. Chandelier bush. A strong brew could make a womb vomit a baby. It's good for cramps, her mother had said. It will help bring down a reluctant period. Clean you out good and proper. But it had not worked because Laura learned to hold the noxious green tea in her mouth until she could spit it out. The period never came. You have your whole life ahead of you, her mother said. Drink it. But she didn't.

Her own teenagers are downstairs now. Aidan is seventeen; Sonia, nineteen. Aidan's girlfriend, Ivy, honey-coloured and wholesome, is there as well. They are baking a cake for her, to cheer her up. Later they will all walk to the other side of the island for a swim. When she turned sixteen, her mother baked a cake and gave her a ruby ring, July's birthstone. Mark left for school that September. Laura had been due to go as well, but all that had been cancelled. Her mother was only forty-six, still young enough to have a baby and heavy enough that no one doubted the pregnancy. Her father had closed his practice and taken up a temporary locum job in St Kitts, moving the family there until Jeannine was born. Her mother delivered Jeannine in Laura's bedroom. Laura laboured for a full day and a night on the flowered shower curtain that her mother placed below her, the pains sawing her until she split in two, as the baby slipped into her mother's waiting hands. Now there were two of them. In that small room so long ago, she'd seen her mother's face change as she held Jeannine, seen the longing.

Once years later, after Mark and Laura were married, they'd gone to Tobago on holiday. Sonia and Aidan were little things. They'd stopped at the famous mystery tomb of twenty-three year-old Betty Stivens. *She was a mother without knowing it, and a wife without letting her husband know it, except by her kind indulgences to him. 1783.* What does that mean, Mummy? Sonia asked her again and again. Could you be my mother and not know it? No, baby, of course not. That's why it's a mystery tomb. But she couldn't get Betty Stivens out of her mind. Maybe she had not been as lucky as Laura, had not had a father as a doctor and a nurse as a mother. Maybe she'd never lived to see the child. Maybe she'd laboured to death in some dark room on her own. It's like a riddle, she'd said to Sonia, and no one knows what it really means.

Mark never knew. Only Laura had been left with her split self and a new sibling. By the time, he'd come back, it was too late to tell him. How could she? And how could they take Jeannine from her parents? Even after she'd had Sonia, then Aidan, she still glanced at Jeannine out of the corners of her eyes. When her parents were killed in an accident, coming home one weeknight, after a Chinese meal, it was all too late to tell. Now she is the only one who knows.

Later that morning, they walk to the calm side of the island. Mark leads the way with the teenagers –Sonia, Aidan and Ivy. To get to the leeward cove, they walk in single file. The path is flanked by wooden posts painted with creosote. At the beach, the teenagers settle on volcanic rocks that ring the protected bay. Sonia and Ivy spread their towels on hardened lava, flat and smooth. When they lie back, their breasts fall to their sides, straining against the thin bikini tops, the bright flash of a navel-ring on Ivy's stomach. Aidan is looking at Ivy from under lowered lashes. Laura remembers the teenage dance, the game of limbs tangled under water. Aidan opens his tackle box and iridescent lures tumble out. As he works, he glances at Ivy, who is lying with a thin arm thrown over her eyes, exposing childlike ribs. He baits the rod, the line arcing in a silver flash over the water.

Laura is ashamed of her swollen stomach, her veiny thighs. Her leaky body feels old and sad as she settles on the beach, panting slightly and breathing through her mouth. Like an old dog. She sits on the folding chair and puts her feet up on the cooler, her eyes closing in the heat, dozing under the blue sky, her eyelashes filtering rainbows. Jeannine settles next to her, gathering her heavy hair up and into a ponytail. Laura senses her leaning back, turning her face up to the sun. She wants to remind her to wear sunblock, especially on the star-shaped birthmark that always burns. Instead she thinks of how she can phrase her words.

"Did Mummy ever brew a tea when you had cramps?" Laura is drowsy but she takes care with her words.

"Chandelier bush? Once, I think. It tasted it terrible. I was sixteen or seventeen," Jeannine says. "We can send the kids to find some. I'll brew some for you tonight; it might help clean you out. Get rid of all that bad blood."

When she opens her eyes, the sun is lower in the sky and Jeannine is drawing a map on a napkin and pointing to the cliffside. Aidan stands watching, drops of water beading the small of his back.

"Pick as much as you can," Jeannine calls as they leave.

Late afternoon comes, and they have not returned. Jeannine, Laura and Mark mill around the beach, reluctant to leave. But they are old enough to know how to get home. They are probably at the house waiting.

When they arrive, the house is silent in the gloom.

Sonia's slippers are at the bottom of the stairs, her bikini drying on the line. She, at least, has come back. Just behind the mountain, the new moon is rising, a fingernail sliver of light.

"They didn't go in the boat," says Jeannine looking out the window. "Even the skiff is here."

On the water, the boat is secure on its mooring.

Mark changes his clothes upstairs. When he comes down, he's picked up a small torch and a whistle, passing without touching her. From the jetty she sees where he is going. He is climbing the path to the whale house. Has he forgotten the channel in the side of the cliff, the hidden passage that runs to the heart of the island?

Standing outside, Laura imagines swimming. Under the thin moon, the plankton are glowing, shimmering like something alive in the water. Behind their island lies larger Chacachacare, with the decaying buildings of the abandoned leper colony. Its lighthouse, still powered by an ancient cogged wheel, floated on a circular bed of mercury. She's stood here many times, under the copse of trees. She counts thirteen seconds before the beam sweeps the bay. Through the trees, perhaps there is the flicker of a candle throwing shadows on the wall.

In the rainy season, water runs off the land and cascades into the crevice, flattening the wild orchids that cling to the rocks and making the brackish water sweet. The water appears just beyond the trees, the crack in the seamless wall of cliff only visible if you know where to look. Laura unties the skiff, sliding the oars into the sea. She manoeuvres the little boat into the stream of water, rowing hard against the current. She rows for ten minutes more, sweating now, and pulls into an alcove with three small steps. Two coconut trees mark the spot and she ties the skiff to the first tree. The climb is not long but she is winded by the time she reaches the top. The whale house has not changed much. It still stands under the silk cotton tree, its windows shuttered and closed. When she pushes open the door, they don't see her. They are up under the window where the light is green and dim. Aidan is between Ivy's spread, honey legs. Ivy sees her first and makes a strangled cry, trying to push Aidan off and cover her breasts. Aidan climbs to his knees and turns to the door. Behind him, she catches a glimpse of Ivy, the pubic hair waxed to a tiny strip above the neat pink slit, the centre moist and slick. Aidan's face is shocked, moon-like in the dim light, his pants around his knees.

Chuck-wit-wit-wee-o, the rufous nightjar calls as she closes the door and runs down the path. Is this what her father saw? When she looks back, they have blown out the candle. Someone else can row the skiff home. She is tired. After a few minutes, she veers off the path and lies down on the beaten earth. She does not think about the giant centipedes that live on these rocky islands, hiding under leaf litter. She is too tired to think of them. Far below, she hears the sea as it bucks past the girdled entrance.

"Laura?" Mark is standing over her.

The light from his torch had alerted her, but she stayed silent until he rounded the corner and saw her. She can see he is torn between worry about Aidan and Ivy and his desire to hold onto his anger, which he dares not voice to her.

"They're in the whale house," she said.

In the way of marriages, the unspoken flits between them. She had not wanted Jeannine in the beginning. But that had changed. And it would have been the same for this baby. Baking cakes is not the way you throw a baby away.

"You think I did it deliberately. You do. But you're wrong," she said.

In a moment she is on her hands and knees, scrambling to her feet. She could tell him now. If there was ever a moment, it is now. But he has walked away, switching off the torch as he goes back down the path. There is no one else to row the skiff home so she rests for a while before going to the boat. The hidden water with its sweetish-salt smell rises around her.

At the house, Mark says he will cook dinner. She says she will sleep for an hour. They don't touch but the air is no longer muddy between them.

She is still sleeping, deeply and dreamlessly, when Jeannine comes into the bedroom. She wakes Laura with soft strokes along her back.

"Wake up, it's after ten," Jeannine says softly, the room chill with sea air. "This will make you feel better. It will help bring everything down."

Jeannine has brewed a batch of Chandelier bush, mamba green in the clear glass. In the dim light, Jeannine's eyes are liquid. She climbs into bed with Laura, pulling the covers over them both. Laura's firstborn is in bed with her. The smell of the tea is the memory of a mother's suspicion, a mother's blame. I don't understand, her mother had told Laura. This baby wants to be born.

"It will clean out whatever is left," Jeannine says, trailing her fingers over Laura's forehead, making the shushing noises Laura's mother always made when they were sick.

Before midnight, Laura is doubled over with blinding cramps. On the jetty below, the nightline is ringing. Something big is fighting the hook.

"Laura!" calls Mark.

"What is it? What did you catch?" she answers him, matching the excitement in his voice. She knows they will never speak of the baby again.

The memory of the nightline comes back to her from her childhood; the things that would surface from the ocean! Once, a four hundred pound grouper, once a hammerhead shark with its rows of teeth hidden in its misshapen head, each one rising up out of the black bay, fighting and pulling on the line, the bell ringing and ringing. By the time she's come down the stairs, they've gutted the shark, an enormous mako with a flat wide head and dead, grey skin.

"Come and see."

The rows of tiny sharks are alive, wriggling and squirming in the cavity of their mother.

He stands behind her, pulling her back to his chest and rocking her, his chin on her head.

TROTSKY'S MOUTH

September 2nd, 2006

Petrea Crescent
Charlieville
Chaguanas
Trinidad

Dear Omar,

You must have heard the news by now. It's true.
Bata killed Sara. You never think you are going to
have to type a line like that in your whole life. He
tried to drink Gramoxone but they got to him in
time. He's in jail now. I have been sending meals for
him because I know how particular he is about his
food. The guards have been quite good and sometimes I don't have to line up too long to get the
package to him.

I suppose you're wondering, like the rest of the
island, what the hell happen to Bata that he would
ups and kill his own wife. We never saw it, Omar,
but Hari and I suspected he was beating her. But you
know you can't get mix up in woman and man thing.
They are calling for the death penalty. I know you

are going to say that it could get tie up in court for years and that they have plenty people waiting on death row to hang. But Omar, Sara was an American, and those Americans don't make joke. They're calling for blood. And it's looking like they will extradite him if we don't hang him here first.

You two were never close as brothers, but I don't know who else to ask for help. Do you think you can come down? Christmas is nearly here and I would like to do something for the child. She is only a little thing. She turned seven last June. She's here with us now and it's working out okay because we had her a lot of the time anyway. Shanti doesn't mind sharing her room with her. I don't think they understand what has happened.

It's sad to think that out of all of us – the cousins and we three – it was just Bata and I who stayed on Ma's land. But now, no one wants to have anything to do with us. Hari was harassed at work last week. It's not easy, Omar, not easy at all.

Write me if you want me to tell Bata anything. I can get a letter to him. I know he did a terrible thing but he is still our brother. Give our love to Chrissy and congratulations on the new baby.

Your sister,
Soraya

The letter lies open on the kitchen table. She's glad that the sisters have not lived to see this day. Dead within months of each other, Aunty Sherry following Ma into the grave like she'd followed her everywhere else. Maybe that's when Bata had become her responsibility. Maybe she'd missed all the signs that Bata was dangerous because she'd been there the night he was born. There was something about seeing the start of someone's life that blinded you. Covered your eyes like a cataract. Bata was a mound of stretched skin between Ma's panty and bra when the moaning and the lighting of the kerosene lamps had woken her six-year-old self, the spill of yellow light pulling her into Ma's room. She'd opened the door as Bata slipped out in a silky whoosh of blood and water onto the plastic shower-curtain, the one with the big daisies that Auntie used to slide gentle gentle under the ladies' bottoms when babies were coming. Even though Bata was a little thing, he'd frightened Soraya, lying there on the daisies, his body all grey and gluey, a big purple cord trailing behind him into the black hole in Ma. On her way back to bed, she'd whispered in Omar's sleeping ear, You have a baby brother, but Omar never stirred.

Maybe he'll reply now, she thinks, picking up the letter and folding it into thirds and placing it in a white envelope before licking it sealed.

Even though it has only been two months, the grass in front of Bata's and Sara's house is overgrown. She'll have to remember to send Hari over to see to it. She imagines all the clothes hanging quietly in their cupboards, the plates in the sink. Sara's hives with the bees have been moved out and the small production room where she processed the honey is locked. But Soraya has been unable to go in to clear the house. She can't face Bata's shoes, the rows and rows of Bata sneakers that he loved so much, nor go through Sara's smocks, as if the clothes themselves would clamour at her.

Their houses mirror each other and in the early morning sunlight, the front of Bata's and Sara's house seems to smile back at hers, warming itself in the morning sun and leaning into the tall bamboo that creaks in the night. It seems to her a Bata kind of house, the same way he'd throw his chest to the sun and rock back on his heels, a big smile on his face. That's the Bata she chooses to remember, whatever the rest of the family say.

They'd all got a plot of land from their grandmother. The old lady had been smart with money. Made sure all of them got an education and had some land to their name. Amongst all the cousins there were plenty doctors and lawyers. Soraya had her marine biology, but after Shanti was born, she'd begged Hari to let her stay home with the baby. That had been five years ago. Bata was the only one who didn't go to university. One by one they'd all left. Even Bata had tried to get out. He'd signed up for the American army but had come right back with American Sara. She'd always worried about Bata, worried that Ma had indulged him, cooking for him and pressing seams into his clothes for every job interview. Maybe it wasn't Bata's fault that he didn't know how to be any other way. But how many times had she lied for him? Blamed Sara?

September 3ʳᵈ, 2006
Petrea Crescent
Charlieville
Chaguanas
Trinidad

Dear Mr. and Mrs. Stoute,

Please accept my deepest condolences on Sara's death. On behalf of my husband and myself, I would like to say that we want to offer any help we can during this terrible time. I understand that it must be very difficult for you to imagine having anything to do with Roger's family, but we want you to know that we are here for you and for Savannah. At the moment Savannah is living with us and she seems settled, although there are nightmares.

I understand that you won't be coming for the trial. I hope that Sara is at peace now and I am glad that we were able to get her back to her people and her home. Savannah has been asking questions that I am not sure how to answer. Have you given any thought as to what you plan to do with her? While she is like a daughter to us, I think that Sara would want her daughter to be with her own family, to be raised with her own people. She is a bright, cheerful little girl who looks a lot like Sara. I know both of you were against Sara moving to Trinidad to marry Roger, but I would like you to know that you have a beautiful granddaughter here who really needs her family. I am enclosing a picture of Savannah at her last birthday party. There she is, cutting her Dora the Explorer cake. She turned seven on the 22ⁿᵈ June.

Please let me know if there is anything that we can do at our end to help bring relief. But for now, rest assured that Savannah is being well looked after and loved. I know Sara wanted her raised as a Christian. We are practising Hindus but I will see what I can do about having her attend the Anglican Church around the corner.

I hope that we can come to some sort of compromise and work towards healing after this tragedy.

Yours sincerely,

Mrs. Soraya Roopnarine-Singh

Why has she written the word compromise? Compromise. A mutual promise of what exactly? She doesn't want a compromise. She wants them to take the child. Truth is, Soraya is a little afraid of Savannah. The child moves with a composure that makes her seem older than seven. She'd taken the best of her parents – Bata's mouth, long and sensual, his slanted eyes laid on even caramel skin, but she is Sara's child in the way she looks up when called, smiling with Sara's dangerous smile.

The child never asks for her father but she still cries at night for her mother. Soraya would climb into bed with her when she woke with nightmares. In the dark bedroom, with her face sweaty and hot, Savannah would rub her head against Soraya's shoulder. The child's smell, tobacco dry, seemed to come from her hair. It is not their smell; it is the smell of Bata's and Sara's house, coming from the pores of the child's skin.

Savannah is violent in her food dislikes, making little wars on anyone who serves her food she hates. Washing the breakfast dishes, Soraya scrapes the untouched egg on

Savannah's plate into the dustbin. Just the other night she'd tried to make Savannah eat a dish of baigan and had felt herself transformed by Savannah's dislike. You're ugly, the child had said, pushing the plate away; her eyes stayed fixed on Soraya until the plate was removed. She felt she'd almost taken on the spongy density of the purple vegetable in the child's eyes. She's just a little girl, she told Hari afterwards. She's been through hell.

Her Shanti, at five, is chubby next to Savannah. It is not that Savannah is ever unkind to Shanti, but there is something in her long-eyed glances that makes Soraya uncomfortable. She knows Savannah told the police very little, but what had the child really seen? She looks up to see what Savannah is doing now. She's at the window looking out at her mother's lettuce, her face expressionless. The plants are going to seed, and there'd been talk of pulling them up, but nothing has been done. Sara had loved her lettuce. She grew them in raised beds between the two houses, a frilled green sea. She had fought caterpillars and slugs, mixing noxious cocktails of garlic and crushed neem, spraying late into the night. After Savannah was born, Sara had worked in the fields with the baby dangling in a sling. But she was always careful; she never took Savannah near the bees. Savannah had been a perfect baby except for an extra toe on her right foot. A quirk of cell division. Ironic, Soraya told Sara, considering she was the only organic farmer for miles around. Even now she remembers the comment with shame. It was just one of the little stabs that she'd taken at the American girl who'd been determined to make their island her own utopia.

November 19th, 2006
Petrea Crescent
Charlieville
Chaguanas
Trinidad.

Dear Omar,

As I have not heard from you, I am assuming that your letter is delayed or lost. Bata is still holding up. The case comes up next week and we will know one way or another then. I have been able to see him twice and he looks quite well, all things considered. I know you are probably asking how it is that I can still go and see him after everything that has happened. I do it in the memory of our mother.

I asked him the last time I saw him if he was sorry. Did he regret it? Maybe a sign of regret might make the jury more lenient. But Omar, he's not sorry. He's glad he killed her. Makes me wonder what two people can do to each other. She really tried, I know she did. But remember what the old folks always used to say? Marry in your own culture. When you marry outside, you don't know what you are getting. Are you alright with your American wife? What is it with you two boys that you had to be better than everyone else and look to America for your wives?

Remember he is still our brother.

Your sister,

Soraya

"Why did you marry him?" Soraya had asked Sara, not long after she'd arrived in the Trinidad. Sara was sitting on Soraya's bed, running her fingers along the creases of the bedspread.

"Have you ever looked at his mouth?" she said. "He has Trotsky's mouth. I had to have his mouth."

"Oh," Soraya said.

She couldn't imagine Trotsky's mouth, though she knew vaguely who Trotsky was. She couldn't imagine marrying a mouth. Shrinking the whole worth of a person to a mouth.

"You like this Trotsky?"

"I like his ideas. Places like this have so much potential, Soraya. They haven't been ruined like America. This could be paradise."

"And they had no Cubans with Trotsky's mouth? Apparently is real nice in Cuba, too."

"You don't know what you have here."

"Clearly not."

Not long after Sara showed Soraya a picture of the young Trotsky. A young man with a thick upper lip, Bata's mouth, a heavy, sensual Trotsky mouth. Maybe that's how someone became a killer. When you were just a mouth, or a slice of a fantasy, perhaps that's what nurtured some killer gene. But was there such a thing?

After Savannah was born, Soraya and Hari heard the fights coming across the land, snippets of words that blew the carrion smell of violence through their windows. Sara saying she wanted more. And once, coming across on the wind: You are not who you said you were. You lied.

The next time she heard Bata raining blows on Sara, she was sorry for the girl but – and she's ashamed to think it now – she was glad that Sara's utopia was being punctured, glad in a sly way that the beatings had caused her mind to skitter onto something else. Such stupid little girls to leave all the opportunities they were born to, just to fly half way around the world to live with a man who does nothing but swing in a hammock and smoke. But what of Bata? Why hadn't she challenged him? Their men were not wife beaters.

"It's because she's American," Soraya told Hari in bed one night. "She thinks she knows what she's gotten herself into but she doesn't understand."

"Understand what?" Hari asked.

"It's an insult thing with men like Bata. He'll never forgive her for stooping to marry him. It's not what she thinks. She's got it all wrong."

Hari had stayed quiet for a long time. So long she thought he'd gone to sleep.

"What are you trying to say, Soraya? She deserves to be beaten because she is American?"

"Of course not." But really it was something along those lines. Something in Sara's assumption that their world was here waiting to be made into a paradise, which negated everything she and Bata had come from.

"Of course not, how could you think that?" She'd turned towards him in the bed. "Maybe you should talk to him, Hari."

"And say what? Don't beat your wife? No, Soraya. What we should do is call the police."

"You know I can't do that."

And so it had gone.

Many mornings Soraya had stood in her kitchen watching Sara work in the garden while Bata swung in the hammock under the tree, smoking cigarettes. She'd watched Sara work through the whole pregnancy. Had helped her choose Savannah's name. They were sitting over a book of baby names when Sara had asked Soraya about Bata's name.

"How come everyone calls him Bata and not Roger?" Sara asked. This was just before Savannah was born. The girl was swollen with hormones, her wedding ring cutting into her flesh. "I thought I married Roger. It's strange when you don't know your husband's name."

"He loved his Bata sneakers when he was a little boy," Soraya said. "He wore them to bed. The name just stuck. He's always been Bata. Bata Bullet, like the sneaker."

Dear Mr. and Mrs. Stoute,

I am sure that by now you have heard the news that Roger has been sentenced to death. I have no doubt that you are relieved at the verdict brought back by the jury. I can understand your feelings. What is difficult for me to understand is how you can turn your back on your own flesh and blood. When I received your letter saying that you wanted to have nothing to do with Savannah, I was shocked. Can you not find it in your hearts to look past all the pain and offer this child a home? I believe it is what Sara would have wanted.

Sara never spoke much about her life before Roger. She never cooked the foods of her home. She adopted us totally, as if there had been no life before here. But I refuse to believe that the ties between parents and a child can be so easily severed. She told me that you were against the marriage because Roger was black. For your information, Roger comes from a heritage of Chinese, Indian, Carib Indian, Portuguese and African. Please do not judge your granddaughter on the colour of her skin. Once again, I am enclosing a picture taken one month ago. Here she is playing with my daughter, Shanti. I am happy to say that she is going to Sunday school and works very hard at understanding her religious primer. I hope that you will reconsider your decision and also find it in your heart to have some compassion for the loss this child has suffered. Roger can never undo the horrific act he committed and for this he will pay with his life. But the child has done nothing. She was her mother's joy.

Yours in good faith,
Mrs. Soraya Roopnarine-Singh

The Trinidad Newspress
18th February 2006
Story filed by Ian Browne – Crime Reporter

It's hard to hang a man on a Caribbean island. Not physically difficult. In that way, it's the same as anywhere else in the world. You tie a noose around a man's neck and then push him off a solid surface. If you are so inclined, you might speculate as to whether humidity could play a part in how a man might slip in a noose were his skin to be damp and slippery. These are idle thoughts. But to hang a man legally on our island, that takes determination. Tired lawyers exhaust appeals to the British Privy Council. Lengthy arguments are laid out before bewigged lawyers in London. They fight, these lawyers, as if their own lives depend upon reprieve. So it is not often that the state places a man in the gallows and legally terminates his life.

But at 4.00 am this morning, a light drizzle fell on the heads of the small crowd who gathered quietly outside the Royal Jail on Frederick Street in Port of Spain to bear witness to the capital punishment of convicted murderer Roger "Bata" Roopnarine. Some carried candles while others clutched small pictures of murder victim Sara Roopnarine. By 6.00 am, the crowd had swelled all the way north to the Savannah and three doubles vendors were doing a brisk trade. Inside the gallows room of the state prison, Roopnarine, slipped through the trapdoor and exited this life. Outside the prison, the crowd slowly picked up a communal prayer, their voices hushed in the early February light. Not long after 6.30 am, the doctor's car was seen leaving the compound, followed by a white-panelled van.

The murder of American citizen Sara Roopnarine has held the attention of the public for close to six months. The young American came to Trinidad as Roopnarine's bride in the late 1990s and lived with her husband on the family compound in Charlieville, Chaguanas. Sara Roopnarine became well known for her organic farming and her pioneering work in meliponiculture. She was a popular figure, driving around Port of Spain and San Fernando in her van with its smiling bee logo and was the recent recipient of the Female Entrepreneur of the Year Award for her work with indigenous bees. Mr. Roopnarine was not known to be a violent man and members of his family claim that he was a man who loved his wife and daughter and have defended him, calling this act of violence "inexplicable".

On the morning of Tuesday September 19th at approximately 8.15 am, the police received a call concerning domestic violence at the family home. Upon arrival they found Sara Roopnarine slumped over the wheel of her van. Mr. Roopnarine was found in the residence with a bottle of Gramoxone mixed with a red Solo soft drink. The couple's young daughter is presently in the care of close relatives and receiving state counselling. Mr. Roopnarine will be laid to rest in an unmarked grave on state land. This is the first hanging to be conducted in Trinidad and Tobago since the hanging of the infamous Dole Chadee and his gang on June 5th 1999.

18th Feb 2006
Petrea Crescent
Charlieville
Chaguanas
Trinidad

Dear Omar,

There is large picture of Sara on the front page of the paper today. It's a blow-up of the small passport photo taken when she'd first arrived. American Sara, fresh from the States with her boxes of Tampax and a six-pack of deodorant as if she thought we all lived like savages on the island. On page two, there is a picture of Bata. Do you remember the day he had the picture taken? You both woke and dressed early to go to the embassy for your American visas. When was that? Do you remember? It was Christmas time because the cane-arrows were up. But how many years ago? At least ten. In the picture his face is calm. He doesn't look like a killer. You can't beat Chinese blood for good skin. It must have been that smooth skin that first caught Sara's eye. Her parents thought that Bata was black. Do you get that over there in Connecticut? We thought maybe it was because he was in Georgia. He told me he never knew he was black until he went to the States. Americans aren't interested in a laundry list of ancestors. To them it is the same; you not white, then you black. I guess I'm telling you all of this now because Bata is dead. They hung him this morning.

He was your brother. You never even asked how he killed her. He locked her in with the bees.

Your sister,
Soraya.

Soraya writes this last letter to Omar in a rush without her usual care, her pen making little stabs on the page. Then she licks and seals it. After she has done this, she calls Hari on his cell. There is nothing more you can do, he says. It's over.

When Soraya imagines Sara's America, the image is based on Sara herself, with her cornflower blue eyes and thick blonde hair. Soraya imagines her growing up in the bible belt of America from people as solid as corn. But she knows enough to realise that this image is as bad as Sara's presumptions about their island. But try as she might, she cannot pin down an image of the invisible parents who have let a daughter and granddaughter disappear halfway around the world. The embassy had contacted them after the murder. They had her information on file. Sara always said they were religious people. Holy Pentecostals. But they refuse to acknowledge Savannah. How do they justify themselves? Was it the same thing she'd heard Ma say about Bata? That bad blood could not have come from her people – it had to come from their father, a sagaboy who'd shared his seed in every village from here to Port of Spain. It was a good thing Ma had Auntie Sherry because their father had not helped raise them. Ma had kicked him out not long after Bata was born.

Savannah was with Soraya and Shanti on the morning Bata killed Sara. There'd been a strong breeze and the bamboo had been creaking as it leaned away from the wind. Then Soraya had heard an animal sound, a raw keening cry from Sara. It sounded like nothing Soraya had heard before and it was this that drove her to dial the police even before she called Hari. In that moment she understood that it had all been leading to this point and she had chosen to look away.

She had called the police without even going over to investigate. When the police arrived, Sara had escaped to the van. She was dying. Bata confessed he'd locked her in with her bees. It was only later, at the autopsy, after the pathologist got the last of the bees off her swollen face, that they realized Bata had bitten Sara on the cheek. Soraya imagined Bata's Trotsky mouth closing on Sara's skin, the sensual upper lip pulling back from the teeth. Everyone said they'd seen it since he was a little boy, that streak of violence. Always a bad seed, her mother said. How could she not have seen it? But Soraya had not seen it and this frightens her almost as much as the murder. The fact that she'd read it all wrong. She'd always blamed Sara.

On the small gallery the two girls sit playing.

"Hi Mama," says Shanti, shifting closer to Savannah.

Little shafts of light hit the undersides of the breadfruit ferns and bounce off the Dieffenbachia plants at the end of the covered porch. Dumb cane. Soraya has been meaning to move them outside, but they are beautiful there, loving the morning sun and rewarding her with fat healthy leaves on solid, sturdy stalks. Last week, she'd taken Savannah to the plants and showed her the leaves. It will kill you if you eat it. Do you understand? Remember it, Savannah, she'd told her. Do not touch it. I've showed it to Shanti as well. She knows too.

As she walks out to them, Soraya folds the newspaper so that Sara's face is hidden.

"What are my two girls doing?" Soraya holds the newspaper tightly against her breast.

"Hi Aunty," Savannah's voice is bright. "We're cooking."

What does she know? They've worked so hard to protect her.

Savannah arranges her leaves in neat piles. Three piles in front of her and one behind her. Shanti chooses from each pile and tosses the greens together in two yellow enamel bowls. Then Savannah picks delicately from the bowls, layering each leaf individually, her attention to detail reminding Soraya so much of Sara. It's good to see Savannah play. Both children are still in their nighties, their feet tucked under them. Soraya automatically scans the ground for danger; for misplaced knives, stray bottles of insecticide, random scorpions.

"I'm just in the kitchen," Soraya tells them. "If you need help with your recipe, I'm right here."

In the kitchen, Soraya is chopping onions when she hears an insistent note in Savannah's voice. It is loud enough to catch her attention. Soraya turns off the radio to listen. Eat it, Shanti. Soraya tries to remember the leaves she'd seen in Shanti's bowl. There'd been a mix of grass, still dewy, and palm fronds. Nothing brightly coloured, no red berries. But had she looked closely enough? There is a cruel insistence to the voice that makes Soraya move quickly.

Savannah, her hair electric and backlit in the morning light stands over Shanti.

"Chew, like a good girl. Eat your salad," says Savannah.

Savannah bends to place another spoon of the chopped leaves into Shanti's mouth.

"Spit it out, Shanti. Spit it out now."

Both children turn to face her. Shanti's face is openly fearful as she chews, Savannah's closed and sullen as she turns to walk away. Dumb cane. It makes the tongue swell. First she won't be able to talk and then Shanti will stop breathing. Soraya's fingers swoop and spoon the leaves out of the child's mouth.

"Spit," she says. "Spit as hard as you can."

The plant milk is acrid on Shanti's breath, her lips already fattening and thickening, the tears coming quickly.

"Shanti, did you swallow any?"

The child shakes her head at Soraya.

"Savannah!" Soraya calls.

Soraya raises her voice until it is stretches high and tight. "Savannah, come here!"

Soraya drives through a haze of tears, one hand on Shanti, who is rubbing her mouth with a towel. In the backseat, Savannah looks out of the car window.

"You knew! Did you forget? You're a big girl, seven years old!"

She never asks the girls who picked the leaves.

In the emergency room of the health centre, the doctor is a young resident.

"Dumb cane. Do yourself a favour and destroy that plant. That's what I tell everyone with children. They can't resist it."

"Mama," says Shanti, pulling Soraya's sleeve. "Mama."

"Yes?" Soraya is dizzy with relief.

"Look, Mama, outside the window. Savannah is eating."

She has unpacked a container from her backpack. She sits, alone at a concrete table with a blue umbrella, her long Trotsky mouth chewing with care. From where Soraya stands, she sees each leaf, arranged like the fancy salads in expensive restaurants.

MAKING GUAVA JELLY

The girls have been eating guavas for weeks. Guava jams, juices, stews, tarts with latticed pastry; each day the kitchen is misty with the perfume of guava. It is the largest crop in years;, the branches obscenely laden, bending under the fruit, the bark mottled and peeling. Nana always believed the dead came out at night to eat guavas. Guayabas, she'd called them. She'd said her own grandmother, Rosa Enrequeta, an Amerindian from the mainland, had told her the stories about Maquetaurie Guayaba, the guava king and his roving band of souls. Over the last week Elise has looked for him every night in her dreams, this handsome king of the Taino underworld, who has no business appearing in a Port of Spain suburb.

Alone in the kitchen, the bones in her back shift and move. Is this how it started? This sensing of your bones, imagining the cells sending out white roots? She places a mirror on the far wall of the kitchen. A hand-painted Peruvian mirror that matches the terracotta floor and the Tibetan bowls that line the counters. The eastern wall is lined with photographs of carnivals gone, ole mas, Minshall mas, bikini and beads mas, photographs of her mother, one of her grandmother, two of the girls as babies, her wedding photographs. Has she flown in the face of some vengeful God? Has he abandoned her because now she only dreams of Maquetaurie Guayaba?

In the mornings the tree greets her even though she is not alone in the house. Maya and Natalie lie asleep upstairs in their beds, faces turned to the cracks in the curtains, pink eyelids filtering the first morning rays to their dreams. She wonders what they dream. Today the clock on the digital stove flashes red, hurrying to tell her that electricity has been interrupted while they slept. She reaches under the island in the centre of the kitchen and unclips her secret drawer. Until six months ago, it had held precious things: velvet boxes filled with the girls' baby teeth and soft locks of newborn hair. The drawer whirs open and slides onto her lap. For the next hour Elise sits looking at women's breasts until she hears the girls stirring upstairs. The images, hidden between the red velvet cupcakes and the meringue recipes in the old Betty Crocker cookbook, are luscious; some caramel-tipped, or tinged with mocha and tinctures of vanilla; others loosely held in frothy lace, delicate as a Pavlova. Each feed an appetite as voracious as any she'd ever known. Today, Elise lingers on her favourite, a lucky find in an old *Playboy* magazine.

John found the lump six months ago, on Carnival Sunday. They'd been looking at Dimanche Gras on television, the blue light of the screen flickering in the dark. On the stage, the Blue Devils shook their pitchforks and baby dolls towards the camera. While John ran his hand lazily over her flesh, she'd followed the invisible map of arousal, turning so the nipple rose against his palm, the feeling delicious under the roar of the city calling *J'ouvert!* When his whole hand had engaged, probing and pressing, she'd known instantly, turning away from the screen as if the Devils and the Dame Lorraines were implicated in her tragedy. She put her hand over his, her fingers pulling his hand away so she could feel. Let me, she wanted to say, suddenly claustrophobic with panic. The lump had been small and hard but it ran roots deep into her chest wall. If she imagined her breast as a clock, the lump was a giant two. It was the breast with the creamy birthmark. When she was pregnant, the mark had stretched and darkened as she grew. Even after she'd had Maya, it remained a heavy question mark on her skin. She'd had the most milk on the whole maternity ward, her breasts filling and leaking to the sound of the nursery wails, the milk running in rivulets down her sides to pool in sticky patches along her body. The girl in the bed next to Elise asked for advice, crying over her own cracked nipples and listless milk.

A week after Carnival, after all the glitter and beads were swept from the streets of the city, the surgeon reached behind her clavicle deep under her arm and her breast was cut from her chest. Afterwards, John told her a nurse passed him on the stairs with the breast in a bucket. He'd cried when he told her this. When she asked her doctor what her breast was doing on the stairs while she lay breathing deeply under the canopy of anaesthetic, he shrugged in the noncommittal way of doctors. It had been on its way to pathology. She imagined her breast waiting patiently, covered decorously in muslin like freshly made mozzarella. Imagining her flesh in a bucket, she had to rest her head on the cool tiles of the kitchen island and count ten backwards to zero to slow her racing heart. Under her shirt, the scar was puckered and knotted, wrapping its way along her ribs.

At first, the images of breasts satisfied the want of missing flesh, a magical game of phantom pleasures. Her chest was still stitched shut when she cut the first breast from a *National Geographic* magazine. The appetite had come with the intensity of lust. The first photograph was one of

111

African girl-breasts tapering to pointy nipples, bare under a collar of rings. She placed each new picture on her new hard chest, pinning the thin paper to the hollow bra, the mirror reflecting her, but not her bald and thin. In her dreams, she felt the weight of the breast on her ribcage. She'd always felt balanced by the two matching globes of flesh that stopped her from listing to either side. Now, she looked at other women in the grocery, imagining the shape and form of flesh that lived in broderie anglaise or white cotton. She pictured herself sliding behind these women and cupping healthy *other* flesh, stealing it away.

"Six centimetres with partial attachment to the chest wall," said Dr. Shah, the oncologist, when she went to see him after surgery. Behind him, a computer screen lit up with the mammogram image of the lost breast, the dark shadow stippled with galaxies of pinpoints.

"Like this," said Dr. Shah. "Walk your fingers up the shower stall. March your fingers until the arm is above your head."

He showed her how to stop the lymph fluid from gathering in her arm. From behind his desk, pictures of Dr. Shah's wife and children beamed down from the bookshelf like celestial well-wishers. Mrs. Shah was pretty with a wide mouth and Elise wondered what her breasts looked like. She thought that at night Dr. Shah must reach over his sleeping wife and gently palpate them, running his fingers in line with the mammary ducts, each fingertip alert to a buckle in the flesh. Elise imagined Mrs. Shah sleeping soundly, breathing in and out, while her husband guarded her breasts.

"We have every reason to be hopeful," Dr. Shah said. This was six months ago.

Her treatment plan was laid out in the office, her salvation on a large white and red laminated poster. In the first box, a smiling woman sat across from her doctor. It was hard to tell if the woman had both breasts. A large red arrow directed Elise's eye to the next box. Now the woman lay in a hospital bed, an IV line snaking from a smiling nurse. Above the woman's head, chemotherapy drugs floated in speech balloons, festively decorated with pink ribbons. Some were connected like amateur family trees while others floated off to the side like errant ghosts. Further along, a glamorous hairdresser stood over the shorn hair of the bald woman. Cancer by flowchart seemed pleasant, mildly soporific even. At the end of the poster, the woman waved goodbye, goodbye.

Today, she is teaching the girls to make guava jelly. From the bucket next to the fridge, the smell of the fruit is sweet and rotten, the guavas stacked in an old diaper pail, the breasts hidden from sight. The girls watch as she pares the thin skin of the first fruit: Natalie, gangly and beautiful at thirteen, her breasts still tiny nubs under her tee-shirt; Maya, a rum baba child, sweet brown and only six.

Elise tries not to notice her nails as she peels. Her old nails were smooth and pink; these new nails are horny and discoloured, only halfway up her nail bed, changeling nails that belong on old lady hands.

"We'll boil the skin separately for jelly and, look, we're boiling the insides until they get thick and frothy," she says, curling her fingers into her palms.

On the stove, thick pink froth bubbles over, hissing as it hits open flame, sending out the smell of scorched fruit.

"That's where the pectin lies," Elise says. "It's what makes the jelly set, like magic."

Was this one of the things they'd remember?

"A worm," says Natalie, looking at the naked innards

113

heaped on the counter. Elise has forgotten to tell them about the worms.

"Sweetheart, all guavas have worms." She laughs, even though it is not funny. "A moth lays her eggs on the guava when it's just a little thing; when it's just a flower."

"I don't want to do this any more," Natalie sweeps the halved guavas off the counter into the sink, leaving a trail of small worms and seeds.

"Oh Natalie, come on."

But the girl has gone, slamming the door behind her and Elise is suddenly so tired she can barely stand.

"So what now, Mummy? What do I add next?"

Maya is in front of her, spoon suspended over the sugar bowl.

"Do I pour out some sugar or do we add the lime?" The child is working hard to keep from crying. "Why do we need lime?"

This is the conversation that will carry them away from the dangerous edge of Natalie's fury that has steamed the kitchen windows and blotted the smell of guava. Elise knows that Maya thinks that this will upset her, this blast of fury that has blown a hole in this carefully orchestrated morning, exactly designed so that her daughters will re-member every moment. She knows that this is what has driven Natalie out of the room. But instead of fury, Natalie has left in her wake a terror that is rising like steam off the boiling guavas. Elise is afraid that this will contaminate Maya.

"Baby, when you add the lime, it stops the jelly from being too sticky. And always wash your hands after handling lime; it will fry your hands in the sun."

She hadn't thought it would be hard for a grown woman to find pictures of breasts. But it was. It was very hard because she didn't want the kind of breasts that men wanted. Perky silicone breasts didn't comfort her. Olive breasts with large areolas called forth memories like silver filaments, delicate and bright. She remembers her grandmother, Islette, pulling on her bra in the thick afternoon light of the bedroom in St. Joseph village. Remembers her old-lady breasts, brown in the swirling yellow light of the room, veiny and shrivelled in their tenacity, set like amber across the years.

Two weeks after surgery, they dripped the drugs into the veins on the backs of her hands. No one told her that Adriamycin would turn the backs of her eyes red. That first evening John found the two girls standing in the doorway to the bedroom, Natalie holding Maya's arm so hard that little red half-moons tattooed her skin for days. The girls had been calling her, but Elise was deep in a red fugue, riding wave after wave of nausea that left her oddly euphoric when she emerged. As if her head were only barely attached to her body.

"I've been fighting all day," she said to girls. "But it's not as bad as it looks. Imagine Mummy fighting dragons; it takes a lot of concentration. That's why I didn't hear you when you called."

To prove her point, she Googled images of fighting dragons and showed them how fierce one needed to be to fight a dragon. Natalie tried to roll her eyes before bursting into tears.

"God, how old do you think I am?"

How old do you think I am? Elise wanted to throw the question back at the child. Just how old do you think I am? Okay, okay, John said, when he saw Elise's face. I'm sorry, she told him afterwards. I think the drug is doing something to my mind. Makes me angry with the girls, at you, at everyone.

For weeks, the dragon raged in Elise's fingernail plates and deep in her hair follicles; little violent wars made her hair fall in clumps and her nails go thin and translucent like the nails on movie vampires.

Is Natalie listening on the other side of the door?

"Always remember, cup for cup. One cup of guava to one cup of sugar."

Perhaps they're too young. Has she been irresponsible, exposing them to boiling water, sharp knives, caustic lime and rotten guavas? Be careful. Take care.

"Mama, did a moth leave an egg in you?"

Between Maya and Elise the sugar pours like rain.

"No, my love, not a moth."

After it is over, the bottles stand on the counter, golden and translucent. Elise is tired, her bones pointed under her skin, pushing like eager dogs against her nerves.

"I can clean." The child sways from side to side, hugging her elbows to her body.

"No, go, baby. Go and play, I can manage."

The mirror works now for emergency pantomimes, for times such as this, when she is so overwhelmed she can scarcely breathe. Through the window she sees Maya wheel her bike down the driveway. Maya looks back and waves. Alone in the kitchen, Elise pulls down the blinds and pulls out her paper breast. She and John have not made love in weeks. Can she blame him? Her skin emits a pulsing, chemical smell. Her hair is fuzzy and patchy, a livid bruise still a blue streak across her chest. *Carpe Diem* says her tee-shirt. Above the *Carpe*, she pins the *Playboy* breast. The breast in the mirror is large, the tight nipple a beautiful taupe on the mocha skin that is Elise's colour.

116

Yesterday, she'd donned an old breast for a different fantasy. Old age. But today she is in a different mood. Today she wants to look at herself in the mirror through slitted eyes, eyes half-closed so that her reflection is soft and misty, until the person that Elise remembers as herself stares back.

Once, a long time ago, she'd painted a dolphin for an art competition. She'd won and had her picture published in the papers. When she'd first felt John's skin under her fingers, she'd remembered the painting: the dolphin half in and half out of the water, his body thick and solid with health, the skin on his lower back smooth, slick and dense. In her painting there'd been wonderful sea creatures under the water: angelfish and barracudas and tiny, fernlike crustaceans, like the ones she'd find on the Mayaro shoreline when she was a girl.

"Mummy?"

Natalie stands at the door.

There is a pile of paper breasts neatly stacked and labelled on the counter. They are arranged in order. All the old breasts lie together. There are tapioca-coloured breasts, indigo and mocha, peach and the gentle lavender of blue veins under white. In another pile, there are breasts that look like Natalie's breasts. Small, pert, tight. They look like the breasts she saw growing on her friends when they changed into swimsuits at birthday parties or at the beach. There are other piles. Piles with babies attached to heavy breasts; piles with voluptuous breasts held loosely in lace or being fondled by hands.

She no longer takes the medicine in the fridge. She suspects that this has something to do with the guava tree, but it's impossible to say why she knows this. Maybe this is how people die? Not like they do on TV with their family gathered around them, faces serene and calm. It occurs to her with something like an electric shock that she is dying. She cannot imagine the possibility of her death, the disappearance of her body.

Now, beyond Natalie, beyond the window, on the lawn under the guava tree, she sees her grandmother. She'd been walking with her mother in Mayaro, walking down the bridle path to the beach between the casuarinas – the beach where they rode the horses down to the water – when the old lady had died in the house. She was buried in Lapeyrouse cemetery between the bones of her parents. It was impossible for her to be here.

Elise cries for the guava god, the one she seeks in the darkness of the garden, in the tangled branches of the tree. She imagines him decorated with hummingbird feathers; he's dark haired and so irresistible that she yearns for him and his band of guava-eating souls. Each night she tells John she feels better, tells him the medicine is working, lying as she looks out the window over his shoulder.

Natalie moves towards the fridge, before suddenly, ghost-like, she is at Elise's side. How did she know?

"We'll get through this. We will. I will give it to you every morning," her daughter says. Her small hands with their square nails and smooth palms are competently adult as the ampoule tip snaps. Natalie flicks it lightly to rid it of air bubbles, as Elise has done so many times. To offer her arm, Elise must unpin her breast and watch it ribbon onto the sugary floor.

The next day John poisons the tree, pouring bucket after bucket of diesel onto the roots. The tree rains guavas and leaves for three days and three nights – enough guavas to feed an army of souls. It stops only when they can no longer bear the smell and sound of falling guavas. By Sunday the tree is dead. John fells it with an axe and Natalie blocks Elise whenever she tries to get to the window.

Some nights when Damiana is visiting Mannie, she entertains his family by mimicking the different people who live in the commune where she works. This makes Mannie feel as if he knows them all. Some nights, Damiana pretends to be the English girl. When she is in this mood, she paces up and down the room with small mincing steps, tossing her head. I am here to do the people's work, Damiana says in the English girl's voice. I am here to help the oppressed. Fat chance of her helping anyone, says Damiana, when she can't even keep her room clean and her man fed and cleaned. Doesn't seem to bother her that she's eating my food every day, but I suppose I not looking oppressed. Maybe when you Indian, oppression is different. Whoever heard of a commune with a maid?

The English girl lives next door to the main house with her black American lover, who tells anyone who will listen to him that he is God. Or at least he thought he was God before he met Mr. Kalam. Mr. Kalam thinks he is Malcolm X and that trumps God. When Mrs. Kalam hired Damiana, she'd offered her more money to clean the foreigners' bungalow but Damiana had refused. Mannie thinks that Damiana must sense some danger and that's also why she makes fun of them. Whenever he is around the commune, the air is dense with something that seems connected to the big car that Mr. Kalam drives. It sits parked out in front of the house, a big white Holden Belmont with heavily tinted windows that make it impossible to see who is inside the car. Between the heavily dark windows of his car and the dark glasses that Mr. Kalam wears, Mannie wonders how the man sees anything at all.

Damiana works from 7.00 am to 3.00 pm. She helps Mrs. Kalam wash clothes and hang them on the line next to the guava tree and she cooks lunch for the assorted people who pass through the house.

Even though Damiana turned down the job to clean the foreigners' house, she ends up doing it anyway. She tells Mannie it is because she is sorry for the girl but Mannie knows it's because Mr. Kalam has told her to do it.

The English girl lies on her bed in the heat of the afternoon. She tells Damiana that this is the hour that she cannot bear. This is the hour that makes her long for soft English rain and pigeon-breast grey skies. She actually says that. Mannie's mother, Benita, sometimes listens in on Damiana's conversations and she tells them that the girl's yearning is triggered by her bedroom facing west and because the bed that she shares with her black American lover lies in the beam of the vicious three o'clock sun. Never lie in a bed that faces west at three in the afternoon. These are the things the locals should tell foreigners when they arrive on the island. Otherwise, these are the things that will send them mad.

At Mannie's home in Sangre Chiquito, all the bedrooms face east to catch the gentle rays of the morning sun. Along the western periphery, leggy immortelles filter the afternoon heat. Soon the trees will be leafy and expansive with the rain, silky with new growth. The signs of the rain come in myriad ways. Benita has taught Mannie to listen to the way birds line their songs upon layers of humidity, to listen to the way they push their love-calls into the saturated air with urgency impossible to ignore. That poor girl, is all Benita will say.

The English girl has not made many friends because of the way she has come to this place. When it is her turn to peel the eddoes and grate the tannia for the evening meal, the coarse skin of these vegetables makes her skin itch.

That morning a woman has come from Port of Spain to buy a horse at Mr. Lee Ling's farm and Mannie is asked to put the pretty stallion with the chestnut coat and roan tail through its paces. The woman smokes a cigarette while she looks at the horse canter on a lead line. Mannie feels sorry for the English horse, sweating in the heat, steam fanning out around him in a large plumed circle. Mr. Kalam stands next to the woman, speaking in an urgent voice and occasionally touching her arm. The villagers say Kalam lived in England for a long time and Mannie wonders if that is why his skin is palely sallow, even though he has black hair, kinky and wild, that lifts off his head in excited clumps. Others say his mother was a small islander and his father was a white sailor. Most people in the village know him as a red man, nothing less, nothing more than a common-or-garden red man. See how stupid foreigners could be? Dotish! They look at a man like Kalam and think he's the real deal. But they said this with a kind of pride, with little inflated chests. Imagine, a local red man gone foreign and make his mark on the white people country. Like a dog would pee on your leg. Marking territory. That had to take real stones.

Benita said people like Kalam were to be watched, like you would watch a two-head snake, because is only a matter of time before he eat himself up. Don't watch him in his eye,

Benita tells Mannie. He will hypnotize you and pull you in. Always keep your head down when you see that red man.

Kalam is speaking with the woman now, leaning on the fence and casually stretching his arm along the fencepost, flexing like a cat, his dark glasses glinting blindly. The woman looks briefly at him before turning back to the horse. The stallion is sweating dark patches into his coat, a light foam building between his back legs. The woman from Port of Spain calls out, Can you put him through his paces again? She is a tall, dark-haired woman. Her skin is olive and her thick hair is held back with a wide floral bandanna. Her lips are carefully painted with a frosty pink lipstick and she is sweating lightly in the heat. The horse is breathing heavily when Mr. Lee Ling gives the signal for Mannie to put the animal out to pasture.

Mannie can tell when Mr. Lee Ling is showing off by his extravagant gestures. A little man with a face like a Volkswagen Beetle, Lee Ling's nose is lost in the protuberance of cheeks that match the two globes of his buttocks above little bow legs. He is a man who would be liable to others' mockery were it not for the tiny motes of savagery that float in his eyes. Next to him, Kalam leans into the woman to say something and it is not long before they have climbed into his the white Holden Belmont and driven away behind the black windows.

Arima is not a part of the world where you would expect to see a white piano travelling in the back of a large truck, tethered with black cables that stand out against its smooth finish. The piano passes some of the grooms on the stud farm as they wait to cross the road and open the wooden gates of the stables. Soon the piano has gone, the little pebbles and dust kicked up in its wake settling on their skin.

The sight of the disappearing piano, followed by the white car, disconcerts them for a moment, before the little convoy disappears round the bend like a mirage.

In the pasture behind the stables, Mannie releases the stallion, unclipping the halter from the lead line. This is Mr. Lee Ling's thoroughbred stud, imported from England and carrying in his blood a champion line of proven winners. The stallion has not acclimatized well and has run sulkily, winning just one spectacular derby before lapsing into tropical lassitude. Now he runs to the centre of the pasture, kicking up clods of dense mud in his wake. Mannie wonders why the woman from Port of Spain said she'd come to buy a horse but, instead, has driven off in the car with Kalam.

Mannie lines up everything he knows about Kalam. He has begun collecting information in the random way of casual curiosity but the happenings at this house across the highway do not follow any familiar plot, or imagined tale. Truth be told, it is the mix of white and black skin, the mix of mouths with their Trini talk butting English clip and American twang that has muddied the story. It is his feeling that even though Kalam talks constantly of the fate of the black man, he does not see the grooms or any other workers. He only sees Mr. Lee Ling and others who come from Port of Spain, the black men who speak with American accents and the English white men who speak with their BBC voices. He only sees the people who can give him things.

Just last week, he brought a very famous man to the farm. In England the man is a very well known singer, but here, in Trinidad, he is simply a pale white man with wire-rimmed glasses. Imagine, Kalam had said to Mr. Lee Ling. Look who reach! Just look who reach on your farm. Don't say I don't take you places, Chinee man! Mr. Kalam is Mr. Lee Ling's friend and Mannie often drives to the house with

Mr. Lee Ling to deliver bags of manure. Mr. Lee Ling tells Mannie that the man is trying to teach the people who live with him how to plant things and how to start a farm so they can grow their own food; as if this is not something most villagers do anyway. The people who come to the house are men who don't look like the men Mannie knows – uncles, fathers or brothers; these men come from Port of Spain and they wear town clothes not garden clothes. Mostly they sit in the front gallery and smoke cigarettes, nodding to Mannie as he drags the sacks of horseshit to the back of the house. Damiana tells Mannie that the men are not farmers, they are activists. They still looking for people to actually plant, she tells Mannie.

"You saw the piano pass?"

Lee Ling raises his voice slightly on the word piano when Mannie comes back from the pasture. No. Mannie looks at him as if he is mad. A piano? What piano?

"Kalam singer friend send a white piano all the way from foreign for him." Lee Ling is swaying on his bowlegs in excitement.

"Go quick, they need help unloading it. They don't want it mash up."

Damiana must have sent a message. She would have had Mrs. Kalam telephone the stable for help.

He recognizes the man who comes to pick him up in Mrs. Kalam's small silver sedan as one of the regulars from the commune, one of the followers. The drive takes them across the highway, along the long road with a line of red flamboyant trees in bloom. The house is the third on the left. From the main road, Mannie can see Damiana gesturing with her hands and directing the truck with the piano to back into the narrow driveway. The house is part of a new housing development. It's set back from the road, a square house with windows sliced by the angular burglar bars. The gallery faces the road and there are four fibreglass porch chairs with backs that spread up and out like the tails of peacocks. Someone has planted a row of periwinkles in front of the gallery, but half of them have withered and died.

Damiana says there have been young men lounging around her kitchen all morning but now they are nowhere to be found. Between the truck driver, Damiana and Mannie, they drag the piano through the front of the house. On his way in, Mannie sees the English girl looking out of the window of the bungalow next door. The bungalow is on the next lot over, but there is no fence dividing the two properties.

By the time the piano is in place, the rice on the stove has burned and Damiana must rush to the kitchen and put two more pounds of rice to soak. That night she will tell Mannie how Mr. Kalam came back with the lady from Port of Spain and showed her the piano, sitting at the small bench and banging the keys so that the house filled with the afternoon heat and the rising sound of hysterical notes.

After they have moved the piano, the truck driver leaves and there is no one to drop Mannie back to the farm. The keys to Mrs. Kalam's small sedan have been misplaced and the Holden Belmont has disappeared again. Damiana feeds him a good lunch of pelau and coleslaw made just how he likes it, with raisins stirred into the mayonnaise, but still Mannie must walk in the hot sun to get back to the farm.

No one has told him that the English girl can drive, though when she pulls up she does it too quickly and Mannie has to step back as the car skids in the gravel at the side of the road before coming to a halt a few paces ahead of him. It is Mrs. Kalam's silver car. He tries not to look too surprised when she reaches over to unlock the passenger door for him. Her skin is very pale, her hands long and blue-veined on the steering wheel. She is a jerky driver, riding the clutch, the car bucking when she gears down suddenly from third to first on the highway. The car heaves and shudders and for a moment he wonders if she has broken it.

"Where are you going?" she asks him, without looking at him. He understands from this question that she wants him to take her somewhere, understands that she has pulled herself off her sun-struck bed and followed him deliberately.

Lee Ling will be angry if he does not return to the farm right away and he knows that he must never say that he has climbed into the car with the English girl who thinks that she loves a man who has brought her to the end of the earth. Where do you want to go? he asks her. What else is there to say?

She is dressed in a pair of brown pants with yellow circles and a sleeveless bolero jacket. On her feet she wears a battered pair of Jesus slippers and her toes are painted a pale shade of pink. When she does not answer he asks her again. Where do you want to go?

He wants to feel flattered that she has followed him, but he can see she is not interested in him. He's just the maid's boyfriend, the groom who brings the manure. He tries to imagine how, later, he will tell the story to Damiana, how he will mimic the English girl, but he senses that there is something at stake between them, some term that he is at yet unaware of and unable to negotiate.

He has watched the woman with the other men at the commune. He has seen the way she walks freely among them, ignorant of their lust because she believes herself safe in the shadow of her American man. He has seen her engaged in conversation with one of the men, watched her lean in to make a point with the zeal of the converted. She does not take the cues from Mrs. Kamal or Damiana that men must be treated in a certain way: managed and fed; talked around and herded. Instead, she walks out onto the gallery in the middling light of early evening, when the men sit around with glasses of rum or scotch or puncheon, quietly smoking long untidy joints spitting with seeds. She walks into this scene and sits amongst them as if she is one of them and can talk to them in reasonable tones. It is clear to Mannie that she is unable to smell the bladed heat that pulses off these men as they smoke and drink and watch her. At the heart of it, they all know it is the schism of *foreignness* that makes her behave in this way. Mannie understands that her man will praise her for her behaviour, believing that she is teaching the men something about equality. He has seen her pinch her skin and pull it until it turns an angry red. I am ashamed of it. I want to be like you, she is saying. She is doing something that no local white woman would do and for that her foreign boyfriend will praise her, Mannie thinks, misunderstanding the unspoken paths that govern the lives of people who live here. Everyone knows that island white women are to be hated, but even they understand the rules for navigating men. Damiana has told Mannie that the English girl and the American black man, who once thought he was God, enjoy wild sex. She has overheard the men talking when she was at the back of the house killing chickens for lunch. She tells Mannie that the men talked in loud voices about what the man likes to do to the girl and how she bends over for him.

Driving next to her now, Mannie is embarrassed for the girl, ashamed to look at the way her short, boyish haircut exposes her face.

"Can you take me to your mother?" she asks. For the first

time, she turns to look at him and the air in the car is suddenly still and silent. The radio is playing "Sunshine on my Shoulders". Do you know they are organising a private plane to go to Haiti this weekend to see a cockfight, she tells him. I'd like to see the birds fight. But there is no room for me on the plane.

She talks while driving, now more slowly and carefully. She tells him that she is quilting a bedspread and she works on it every night. Mannie wonders if she is mad.

Why do you want to see my mother, he asks, even though he knows very well why she has followed him out onto the main road in the silver car. The English girl must want to know her future.

Aiye-yaie-YAIE! Mannie, where you going with whitey-pokey? I never take you for a man who like white meat, shouts a man from the crowd lounging on the bridge below the church. Mannie throws his hand out the window, flinging his wrist back. Hush yuh ass, panyol.

"What did he say?" The girl is concerned. Nervous. Her ears deaf to the words but not the tone.

Nothing, he tells her, but in his mind he is wondering what his mother will say when he pulls into the yard with this pale white woman. White cockroach skin.

"Does your mother have bones?"

"What kind of mad-ass question is that?" For the first time he is alarmed and looks closely at her. She keeps her eyes on the road.

"Doesn't she do that thing? Shake the bones?"

"What thing? And no, my mother does not shake bones." He knows she is referring to his mother's reputation as a seer woman but he's not going to make it easy for her. Was his mother an obeah woman? He didn't think so. What she knew she knew from her mother and her mother's mother and long before that. No talk of corbeau peeing on your head or jengay or all the other things people say mark an obeah woman. It wasn't like that. What his mother did was different. He'd watched her, watched her collecting her herbs in the magic hour between dusk and night, careful to throw back some leaves for the spirits. He was familiar with the leaves suspended in bottles of liquid in a corner of their kitchen. When he'd had fever as a child, she would measure the drops into his mouth, using the eyedropper from the blue bottle of Optrex that his father kept in the bathroom.

"What thing?" he asks again. Wanting her to say it.

"See into the future?"

"You can ask her when you get there."

"I've brought money."

"If she sees you, she will want you to make a donation at the church where the Capuchin monks are buried."

People said that his mother chose to live near the church but he knows that was not so. She had come to take her dead cousin's place and that's how she'd ended up close to the church. Every morning she visited the church in San Rafael and said the rosary, offering prayers for the repose of the souls of his dead half-brothers. She never said it, but he knew she confessed every time she prayed, believing her gift to be the devil's work. How does it happen, he'd asked her once. Easy, she'd said. Like a movie. Sometimes they don't even need to ask. Sometimes it's so strong, I can see it when they are walking towards me.

People came from Port of Spain and San Fernando. Rich people in big cars. They wanted to know if their wombs would quicken. Would their husbands leave them? What mark to play in whe whe so they could make millions. But those were not the things she foretold. The things she saw she never told them. Instead she eased out banalities. They don't want to know, she told Mannie. They think they do but they don't.

"What Capuchin monks," the white woman asks.

"Nobody never told you that story and you living on this side so long?"

It was the type of story foreigners loved. He's surprised Damiana hasn't told it to her.

An early war between the native Indians and the Spanish, he told her. Three monks were killed.

"When was that?"

"I forget. Sometime around the end of the 1600s."

"What makes the monks so special?"

"People say when the Spanish went a year later to dig up the bodies of the monks, they were still fresh. Still bleeding. Flesh on their bones good good. Smelling like normal…" Here he paused to look at her. Were you supposed to say these sort of things to foreign women? But she still kept her eyes straight ahead, listening.

"They say it was a miracle. So they make them holy martyrs and move them around a few times. Talk is they going to eventually bring them here, to the San Rafael chapel. I not sure where they are now. Ask her when you see her. She will tell you."

The English girl stays silent, driving around the corners of the road carefully and she asks no more questions.

"Turn here."

"Here?" Her English accent makes the word sound more proper as if her here and his here were two different places.

They drive slowly down the long winding driveway. Past the big starch mango tree and past the row of bois canot with their oversized leaves. He's pleased that the English girl is seeing where he lives, can see that he's a person with a house and a mother and father and everything is neat and tidy and pretty overhead, with overhanging branches and wild lianas and wild pines sending out flowered spikes high in the trees.

By the time the English girl has parked the car, Benita has come out to meet them. She's still beautiful in her fifties. She's accustomed to white people coming, but no one had telephoned and Mannie can see she's worried to see him in the car with the English girl.

"Ma, this is the English girl who lives by the people Damiana working by."

"Hello, pleased to meet you. My name is Emily-Ann," the English girl says. "Thank you for seeing me." The words rush out of her mouth as if she's afraid she will swallow them.

But Benita will not see her. For a moment the two women look at each other. Benita covers her face with her hands. No, she says. No. No.

There's nothing to do but ask the English girl to get back in the car.

But why? WHY? Why won't she see me?

Benita has locked the door and pulled shut the curtains by time the English girl is turning the car in the yard. When Mannie looks back, his mother has come out the door and is sweeping the path where the car has been with a cocoyea broom, her face down.

The English girl does not say anything for a long time. Then, when they were nearing the horse farm, she says that maybe his mother doesn't like white people. Maybe she doesn't like foreigners. She says what a bad thing it is that people like her came all the way across the ocean to try and help people who had no rights and then these same people are so ungrateful.

Mannie lights a cigarette and exhales blue plumes out the

window. When the English girl lets him out opposite the farm, he slams the car door hard and doesn't look back.

That night when Damiana begins to speak in the mincing tones of the English girl who had vanished all afternoon in Mrs. Kalam's silver car and created panic at the commune because no one knew where she had gone, Mannie leaves the room and Benita asks Damiana to stop. It's unkind. Damiana sulks for the rest of the night, sitting out in the front with a lone kerosene lamp and listening to her small transistor radio. It's only after Benita has gone to bed and he walks Damiana to her home on the main road, that he tells her what happened.

You ever saw your mother do that before?

Never.

What you think she saw?

She doesn't want to talk about it.

Early in the January of the following year, Benita tells Mannie over breakfast that the snake has eaten itself. The two-headed snake would soon be no more.

It was almost a month before the grave was found under the lettuce growing tall and spindly over the mounds of manure that Mannie himself had delivered to the commune. Yes, he tells the police, they kept wanting more. Said they wanted it for a compost heap and to plant. He remembers the day well because the woman from Port of Spain had come to collect her stallion and he hadn't had time to keep shovelling more manure. They had pushed the girl in and killed her. Mrs. Kalam had never heard a thing. Damiana told Mannie she was sure that the girl had gone back to England. All her clothes were gone.

★

It's best in telling a story like this to line up all the people. To place them in their respective corners so that everyone understands what sort of story is being told. It is a story that could be told by Damiana, but how could she know all the details? She's just the maid, a young Indian girl hired to help in the house of a black power activist. Mannie perhaps could tell this story. But what could he bring to it? He is a groom on a horse farm that lies across the highway, who occasionally brought manure to the house.

But the English woman had been able to tell her part of the story in the end. She had been pushed into a hole dug for composting. She'd been alive when they covered her with manure, all the men that she joined in the middling light of evening. When the foreign press had come to the tropical backwater, it had been a circus, though the foreign pathologist was very good at his job because even bones will talk in the end.

Far beyond the ex-pat gaze, the lives of ordinary Trinidadians unfold in ways that foreigners find difficult to imagine. It is a curious blind spot, not unlike the sharp corners on the north-coast mountain road, and no one knows quite what causes people to speed blindly, beyond the reach of their vision. Even though the road signs warn of danger, there are frequent collisions, the casualties mounting with alarming regularity.

On a hot day in the late eighties the bodies of the three Capuchin Monks are moved to their final resting place in the San Rafael Church. On that day Mannie, who is now middle-aged, goes with his mother to light a candle. She struggles with arthritis in her hands now and he must light her candle as well as his own. They never speak of the English girl whose bones now lie with her own people, far across the ocean.

Mannie remembers, though, that when the lady from Port of Spain moved to England she took the stallion with her. Every time Lee Ling saw Mannie after that, he tells him the horse is living a charmed life in the motherland. Lucky bugger.

FLEAS

Now I was dead, I'd forgotten the point of all the swagger. The boys didn't stop to make sure I was dead. Who could doubt death after emptying two clips into a body? It made me sad to see my blood leaking into the dirt. Like my mama had wasted all those years of Ovaltine and vitamins. She always said I was born ready to catch a ball. And no one could beat me on the track. Not in those days anyway. Dawn spent running around the savannah, feeling the breeze rush by. It took twenty-two bullets to slip me out my skin. By then there wasn't much left of anything. They'd missed my face. That's how I was sure it was me, lying there on the black road, the blood pooling and reflecting the street lights. It's true you slip out in the same bloody rush that you arrive in. I did try to get back in. I really tried, but there were so many holes I just kept slipping back out. I was sad for Mama, sad and shame – a leaking dead son from a line of pan men and footballers.

It's not like you think. I never saw no light. Nothing like what those nasty old priests taught us in school. No set of angels neither. I'd nearly died once before. Hoss, the boys on the block said, little soldier, come and try this smoke. The weed choked my throat shut until the veins in my eyes beat that light right in front of me. Looked like an angel. Didn't feel like spirit lash, which is what everyone said after. Told Mama and she said talk to the priest. As if telling him about the light meant that I wasn't rotten. She told him but he said why would an angel appear to a weed-smoking asthmatic? That's why the Imam always liked me. He knew I'd sell it but never touch it.

By that time I was climbing into bed with Angie and sinking myself in her night after night. You're a good boy, she said. Made me want to cry that she knew that I was one of those that held the government hostage for a week and she still let me climb up inside of her. But you're a hero, she said; it just depends which side you're looking at it from.

I was the first one to shoot a bullet, and she still thought I had some good in me. Not the way those doctors looked at you when they were stitching up the bullet holes that the police put in you. Stitching you back up neat and clean, but looking at you like they couldn't believe anybody could have loved you or stroked you or wrapped you up when you were sick. Holding their breath when they had to touch you. But by then I really was going bad. Rottening from the centre.

Who would have thought I'd have the head for numbers? That old priest never saw it, but the Imam did. He'd bailed me out of jail after I robbed the red woman on Henry Street. All that set of bawling and crying for a skinny gold band. I ran but the police were on me like flies on a dead dog. The Imam came the next morning. Said he'd take me to the Mosque. Feed me and teach me how to pray. And he did. Even though, Mama said after, he also showed me how to load a gun and hold a government hostage. It's things like that that make you go bad, she said. But she was wrong. That stink-ass white priest had long covered that ground. I saw some things that week in the Red House, that fancy seat of parliament. Big hardback men crying like babies. I shot the guard at the bottom of the stairs to start the races. Bam. And he was dead. He stayed there for a week. Blew up like a balloon before he began to stink.

They had a special on TV last year. Some documentary that won a big prize in America. All about us. There we were coming out of the Red House with our hands on our heads. Big-time reporters everywhere, whitey whitey and sweating in the rain, wiping condensation from them big lens cameras. But the Gulf war stole our glory. We never got any real credit for it. No real blame either. Everyone just got on with their business. The Syrians built back their buildings. Some more white people left and the Indians began to get serious about getting into government. You didn't need no set of book sense to know that there was easy money to be made. Cocaine like salt. The country could never put a face to us. Like all little black boys look alike. So it was the Imam who took the bounce. Kind of sad if you think about it, because he was probably the only one that really thought he was doing something good. The rest of us were just learning how to kill. And fuck. By then I had three babies on the hill with Angie, sowing them as easy as you seed tomatoes.

The Imam liked dogs. Not the pits and rots that everyone got into. No. He liked the little ones. The pompeks you keep in the house. No one knew that about him. I went to see him last week. Mama would say someone walked on my grave. The way I dreamed him. Go to the water, he said in the dream. You must go to the water. But in the dream, he didn't look like the Imam, even though I knew it was him. He was a white man. Fat and soggy with a deep Southern drawl. Go to thah wahtah, he said in the dream. I knew it was him even though his eyes were blue. A North American blue. Pale and watery. My grandma saved me from death, said the white man Imam. She breathed life back into my body after they'd put me in the ground. So I went to see the real Imam the next day and he said, Boy, look at you. You a big big man now. You better watch your scotch if you know what is good for you. The diabetes had taken a leg by then and he was breathing hard and fast. I had to help him up when he wanted to pee.

The police are here now. Even they are surprised. Bullet casings everywhere, me laid out like an old, leaky sack, bleeding and bleeding. All the grannies out in the street now. People think Laventille is a ghetto. A hell hole, the newspapers say. I wish they could see it now. Miss June has brought out the candles. Why is it always the old who must mind the dead? Behind Miss June is her red ixora hedge with its big red blooms. Miss June and my grandfather used to court, she told me once. He'd beat pan until late and then throw stones at her window.

Mama is here too. Wonder how she feels watching all that blood she grew under her breastbone leaking out down the road. Buckets of blood running like rivers. Just like the prophets called it. It's just not the blood we thought would run. Go to thah wahtah.

Someone is on the phone now. Calling the Imam. Some-body will have to pay for this, I know. Djabès, Soukouyan, lougawou, Zonbi! Evil is lurking.

There is a way you approach playing pan. Not everyone can beat pan. You have to watch the pan. Get to know it.

Oh God, Mama is crying now. All the creole bubbling back up. Kwiyé yon dòktè! Call the doctor!

There is a way to play pan. You have to approach it the way you think about a hard math problem. Like when you're working scaled commissions on different weights. Half the crew wanted to work in ounces and pounds, but all the ones who came after the metric switch only knew about grams and milligrams. Try working commission on that.

139

You have to approach pan the same way. Gather your head and pull yourself together until you can feel yourself poised and waiting in your chest. The pan asks that you sink your legs into the ground and feel for the rhythm to come up from the core. It comes up through your legs and pulses out onto the pan with you vibrating in the middle, like a good fuck or a good set of numbers. Shooting a man never made you feel that way. But for other men it's different and that's why they liked to kill.

Not everyone could roll a note on the pan. But I could make a note roll so long and sweet, big man stand up and cry. One time, a big-time musician come down from Germany. Some workshop thing the government was doing, trying to get us off the street. Well, I drop a roll on that man, just hit him around the head with that note coming up off the pan as if it was rising out of the ground itself, as if the oil from the earth remembered the pan and was calling for retribution.

They have people out there who well believe big word like retribution is not a word that would come to my mind. That I don't have the book brains to know a word like that, but you don't learn about a word like that in school. I used to think about that selfsame word nearly every day. Anyway, I nearly kill that man that day. Big German man sit down and cry. There is a way you approach the pan. Not everyone could make it give up its notes just so.

Now Angie reach. I wonder who she calling? Her mother? Her sister? Her next man? They say pan and woman is the same kind of thing. And I could play both, but in the end it was Angie who was playing me. When I went to see Imam that day, he told me, Watch your scotch, big man. I hear your name getting call all around town.

Is only so much I could do. These are different times. I never prayed with the Imam. I'd sit on the steps and smoke while he prayed. Three times a day. Most times one of his wives would come out and offer me a drink. All the wives, all three, smart, smart.

In the end, he was right, I should have taken a Muslim wife, or two. But I wasn't into all that hijab thing. Under the street light, Angie is crying now. It's too late for the Imam to be praying. He must be asleep. So his prayers can't move me along now. Mama is praying now but she's been praying for a long time. Lighting candles. I never knew she lit a candle for every man I killed. How you know, I asked her. How? How? Who told you? A fos frékanté chyen, ou ka trapé pis. When you lie with dogs you will get fleas. And she would go on lighting her candles.

The boys come from nowhere. Little boys groomed to kill, holding their first guns and sniffing the metal. Couldn't have been much older than fifteen or sixteen. The young boys are the best ones for the difficult hits. Trigger-happy and excited, they love to kill. By the time you get to my age, it's hard to do it. Hard to watch the life leak out of a body and remember your mother's candles. Tonight, the boys were young and faceless. The one who pulled the trigger was small, a little boy, his pee probably not even frothing yet. Little red boy wearing a batman mask and a rastaman wig surrounded by a band of scabby boys toting big guns. They surrounded me, jittery and pumped up, until I thought they'd climb me like cats on a tree. Hey. Hey! Oye. Soldier, soldier. Cool it. You know who the fuck I am?

I still can't believe a little boy wearing an old Machel shirt shoot me. Put the gun in my chest, cool cool, and pulled the trigger BAM. Then the others emptied their magazines, but not one would touch my face.

The police are stripping me. The trophy watch from my first kill. A wedding band from the white woman on the avenue. They turn me over to get my wallet. I'm already stiffening. First I'll stiffen, then I'll go soft. Mama and Angie are wailing. Behind them I see the boy coming. He no longer has on his mask. But he has not changed his clothes. The Machel shirt is still clean, not a mark on the jersey. The boy was good. Someone trained him well. He is behind Mama now. Now they are so far I barely see him hand her the candle. Tonight the village will light flambeaux and the pan will beat for me. Fuck. Far below, I am rotting.

A fos frékanté chyen, ou ka trapé pis.

BRIAN AND MISS ZANANA

Not many people have seen the legendary mapepire zanana close up. Not really close up. That's because mapepire zananas live high in the Northern range of Trinidad. The South American bushmaster. Some people say you can find the largest one in Trinidad sunning on the large rock outside Cumaca Caves, guarding birds and bones. They are beautiful snakes, apricot and cream dappled, but most people only see death when they look at them. People who know say they are slow to move but quick to kill. I had a mapepire zanana as a boy. I caught her high in the hills above Arima. I watched her all day by the river. They like the water. Sometimes they swim, crossing rivers like dogs with their heads held high. I waited all day until night fell and her blood cooled in the chill air. By the time I had the forked stick on the back of her head and my tongs at her midsection, she was slow and thick-blooded, folding into my leather bag as if she wanted to be caught. Not long after, she laid eggs and I was sorry that I did not catch the male. I waited two and a half months for her eggs to hatch. When the neighbours heard that we were nurturing a nest of vipers in the backyard, my mother made me kill them all. This was when we lived in Arima and I could have just as easily released them, but my father skinned her and sold her apricot and cream skin in the market for $500 dollars. I drowned the hatchlings in a vat of kerosene. Only when I got my zoology degree did my parents puff their chests and see some merit in my fascination.

At the zoo, I am in charge of many things but it is the snakes that really hold my attention. I care for a pair of zananas. When I give tours to school children and tourists in the snake house, Miss Zanana and Boyfriend sometimes raise their heads in their glass enclosure and turn to me as if they are interested in what I have to say. The crowd almost always steps back from the glass. I'm the only one in the history of the zoo to have bred a pair of bushmasters, and for this I confess to a modest pride.

"Mr. Brian," Boyfriend seemed to say to me one morning. "It is time. I can taste her in the air."

Boyfriend positioned himself next to Miss Zanana and tongue-flicked her. She uncoiled gently and opened for Boyfriend to insert one of his two penises under her tail. I was embarrassed for them and left quietly. They stayed this way for another four hours before uncoiling. A few weeks after, Miss Zanana laid eight eggs, round spheres bigger than the speckled hens' eggs in the bird coop. Seventy-six days later, the eggs hatched into pretty multicoloured baby bushmasters. The Zoo's newest babies are now twenty inches long and pale, some with bright orange tail-tips and some with yellow ones. It's easy to forget the fangs folded against the mouth-roof of even the tiniest viper.

I don't live far from the small Anglican Church in St. Ann's. Every morning I walk to work through the Botanic Gardens, past the cemetery full of dead Governor Generals, under the bamboo tunnel and enter the small gate at the back of the zoo. I prefer this entrance to the public turnstile. In February, the gardens are lit up with the blooms of exotic trees. The Indian silk cotton tree pushes out hot pink sprays and the pouis bloom yellow and pink up the dusty Lady Chancellor hill. Some days when the trees are in bloom and the nights are cool, I bring Rhonda home with me on the promise to cook for her and rub her feet. On the mornings after, she runs ahead of me through the gardens, her shoes in her hands, yesterday's clothes folded in a brown paper bag. For a while we thought that Mr. Wool had not noticed.

But it was not long before Mr. Wool caught us in the snake house, kissing long deep kisses under the scarlet racemes of the macuna vine. This vine is very famous and people come from far away to see it bloom. I rubbed some of the yellow pollen on Rhonda's face before I kissed her, marking the spots where I would place my mouth. I had already made several tiny yellow moons down her neck when we realised we were being watched. He had come up quietly in the gloom of late afternoon, standing there and staring at us until my skin tingled and Rhonda's nipples hardened against my chest.

I have paid for my involvement with Rhonda: a written reprimand on file for insubordination; a threat to remove me from the snake house. There are many others who need the experience and Brian Roget has shown signs of insubordination. Mr. Wool writes this in his next monthly report to the Board of Directors. Rhonda types the correspondence and tells me the contents of the letters. Did he say anything to you? I asked, but she said that Mr. Wool had never brought it up with her. I pay in different ways, she said. Sometimes I think I smell old man's spunk on her but the smell of zoo stays on all of us and it's hard to tell what we smell is real or imaginary.

Rhonda is not a young woman. I'd never slept with anyone older than thirty before, but Rhonda is only thirty-five with a smooth, flat stomach and maroon nipples. She has a toasty brown skin that sits thickly on her flesh with a sense of assurance and warmth. When she laughs, she throws her head back so that you can look long and hard at her neck. It is these things that make her desirable. The only flaw in Rhonda is what she feels about snakes. I told her once about a glossy-banded coral snake, a magnificent female, that crossed my path one afternoon, running like liquid through the dry leaves on the hill. She said, You could watch and not see they bad? What kind of man could really like all that cold blood?

She has been working for Mr. Wool for fifteen years. She types his letters, listening to his dry voice through the Dictaphone. It is easy to see how a man like Wool with his long-fingered hands and smooth, high-brown skin might once have been attractive to Rhonda. He comes from the type of family that educate their children in foreign and teach them how to eat with the fork tines pointing downward. Rhonda tells me he is a distant relative of the long-dead painter, Cazabon. She says this with the slightest edge of pride. He is a wealthy man with no children.

She's slept with Mr. Wool once or twice. I come to know this late one night, after we'd kicked off the sheets and lie diagonally across the bed to catch the rays of the moon. She's talking and I'm listening to the sound of her voice, listening to the details of Wool and Rhonda, details she wants me to believe are past and irrelevant. While she talks, I try not to think of Rhonda's nipples in Mr. Wool's mouth. I wonder if Rhonda may still sleep with Mr. Wool if he offers her certain favours, but this is not something I want to think about.

Outside the window, a decapitated palm tree holds a woodpecker family and I know we will wake to the tock tock tocking in the morning. What was it Rhonda said when she told me about the letter? I remember. Leave it alone, she'd said. He can be a vindictive man. Then we'd lightened the mood, joking that Mr. Wool thought he would be buried with the Governor Generals in the Botanic Gardens because he believed he was an important man. I thought of how I'd caught Wool urinating in the bushes the previous week. The old man had turned at the sound of my footsteps, his shrivelled brown cock a limp snail in his hand, the urine spraying in a feeble arc. I'd almost not headed off the group of convent girls coming down the path.

This March morning, Ella Ocelot's cage stinks of rank cat, a musky jungle smell. Where is everyone? The boots and the broom are neatly stacked against the ocelot's cage; the bucket of fresh fish sits waiting, the eyes not yet cloudy. Ella paces and paces, throwing irritated glances at me while the bougainvillea draped in the saman tree sheds a gentle pink rain over her cage. Some mornings, on my way in, I hear the lions roaring, deep yowls that stop the stray dogs in their tracks. This morning I'd heard Ella's raspy cries from the bamboo tunnel and quickened my pace because I knew she would be hungry.

Ella is located in South America. The zoo is mapped out like a miniaturised world. It's easy when you enter to walk effortlessly out of Europe into Africa and jump over the bridge into South America. The giraffes for Africa are arriving today, but generally my terrain is South America. I like the loud cries of the macaws and the lazy swoops of the giant otter in his pond. The path to the snake house stays mostly in South America, but with forays through Africa and India. Not only is Ella unfed, her cage is unlocked. That she is pacing with such exaggerated leisurely rolls makes me think she knows this as well. Knows

147

that she could escape if she really wanted to do so. Has anyone missed Mr. Wool?

Rhonda is suddenly behind me, a small entourage of workers trailing her like bachacs. Before I can greet her, she turns away, clapping her hands and motioning the workers back to work.

"Is your cell off? I've been trying to call you." Her pillow mouth is hard, the maroon lipstick bunching on her Cupid's bow.

"I was on my way up, but Ella's cage is unlocked and she hasn't been fed." I reach for my cell phone and turn it on. "Wool must have screwed up."

Ella suddenly stops pacing and fixes her gaze on Rhonda and then looks at me. The woman and the cat stand separated by a thin metal bar and a sheet of fortified chicken wire, the smell of rank rising up between them. The cat jumps suddenly, pivoting with a leap into the tree that stands in the centre of her enclosure. There she lies, panting, eyes half closed in the heat.

"Here." I hand Rhonda the breakfast I've brought her, two doubles, the curry channa wrapped in the floury barra still warm from the vendor. I'd added the cucumber souse and the tamarind chutney she likes.

"Where's Wool? He usually feeds Ella." We both know that the old man likes the cat. In the last few months he'd taken over her morning feed, often dragging a plastic chair to watch her eat.

"I don't know."

I note she is clipping the master set of keys to her belt. We both know these keys are Mr. Wool's and that he keeps them at his home, clipping them to his belt before leaving each night.

"What's going on, Rhonda?" I hear my voice stretching

148

into the long vowels of my country accent, a reverse stutter that can only trip me.

A school tour is due to arrive at ten and I have to clean the snake house before they arrive. I have to check on the snakes. I am the only one who counts the babies every morning. I'm the only one who ensures they are all accounted for. Perhaps I will choose the rainbow boa as the snake of the day and give Lucy, the macajuel, a rest. My snake house is the most popular interactive tour at the zoo and we get good crowds every day.

By the time I am slipping off the boots and snapping shut the padlock on her cage, Ella has jumped down for her fish. Rhonda holds the bag of doubles in one hand and covers her mouth with her other hand. This morning her skin is less buoyant, less fresh. But her hair is combed and her zoo shirt neatly tucked into her pants, the master keys now securely clipped onto her leather belt. Her hair is pulled back from her face. Her eyes are so swollen that the top lid pillows over her lashes so that they look shorter and spikier than I know them to be.

She hands me back the brown bag holding her breakfast before pressing the heels of her hands into her eyes.

"Mr. Wool is missing."

The tears are under the surface of her voice, swimming up at me. Because I cannot see her eyes, I don't know where to look. I look up towards the office and down towards the gate. I cannot say what I expect to see.

"You haven't seen him have you, Brian?" Her eyes are watery, the skin below them slack and pouchy. "You haven't seen anything, Brian, have you?"

I think before I answer her. I wonder whether to tell her that I have seen her climbing into Wool's car late in the evenings when she is not with me. I wonder whether to ask her if she lies across his bed late into the night, telling Wool things about me. I'm trying not to think of Wool at all right now.

"I left you with him yesterday, Rhonda. I left you two in the office."

★

In the peculiar, beautiful light of a March afternoon, the meeting had not gone well. He'd refused to sign off on a standard purchase order for animal feed and bedding deliveries. The conversation between us pushed forward with little stops and starts, the room stuffy with Wool's silent irritation. While we waited for Rhonda to type up the minutes of the meeting, the air between us swayed gently in the mossy light, the room an airless aquarium.

I'd already taken on the bulk of managing the zoo, but would I get the job when Wool retired if he voted against me? Rhonda said it was hard to predict. She said it was hard to say what *her* position would be when Wool retired. Wool had never mentioned coming upon us in the snake house but every meeting since had been punctuated by little ellipses of old-man hostility and jealousy. On this March evening, the air-conditioner had stopped working and we sat in the airless heat, sweating into our seats.

Along the left side of the office, housed in a custom-designed mahogany case, was Wool's butterfly collection. I had never met a serious lepidopterist before Wool. In the case are all my childhood favourites: the Scarlet Peacock, the Owl Butterfly, Cattle Heart, and the Blue Emperor. Each pinned to the board with such gentle dexterity that no blemish mars the long dead wings. Behind the large mahogany desk are several photographs of younger Wool. There's a photo taken of him in the '70s – a picture he must have liked a great deal. In the photo, he could be a young

150

Jimi Hendrix in big sunglasses and a bright paisley shirt. Next to him is someone who looks like John Lennon and, further along, someone who might be our first Prime Minister. At the side of the photograph a white woman smokes a cigarette, the smoke obscuring her face.

I left Rhonda packing up and the old man working at his desk, the low-lying sun casting a sallow glow on Wool's face, throwing the old bones into relief.

★

From Ella's cage, I can see the snake house. It sits on a bluff that overlooks the duck pond. You can't see the sign above the door – it says: *Welcome to the Snake House. Shhhh.* I reflect that Rhonda and I have been meeting once or twice a week in the snake house but I'd never asked where she sleeps when she does not come home with me.

When I'd arrived four years before with a degree in zoology, she'd been there, typing letters and running the office. The resident brown sugar. Everyone knew she was sweet like molasses, thick and rich on the tongue. In the beginning she'd worn a gold ring with a tiny diamond, waving her hand to throw rainbow prisms. One morning, she'd come to work with a naked finger and the early signs of an arching back. I nearly missed it, all that back-arching and head-tossing, but when she'd begun leaning in closer, I learned her smell, learned to taste it on my tongue. I first kissed her in the back row of the cinema, running my hands under her blouse and reading her flesh like braille, searching for the sugar granules that I was sure coated her skin. With each kiss I'd inhaled her, the notes coming in layers – baby powder and jasmine perfume on a sturdy bottom of yeasty female smell.

"All that cold blood," she used to say when I told her how much I liked snakes. "What man could like cold blood?" All the while her finger would be gently pressing the cordy veins on my hands. I never flinched at the bubbly feel of blood stopping and starting.

Behind Rhonda, Ella resumes her pacing. When Rhonda turns away from me, her back is rigid, a line of sweat tracing the outline of her spine on her shirt.

"What you mean he is missing?" I am having difficulty keeping up with her pace, but can tell she is heading to the office. "How long?"

"He didn't come in this morning and he didn't sleep in his bed last night."

Wool's disappearance is hovering over us like a fine mist.

"Where could the old fool have gone?" I ask her. "What is it, Rhonda? What's going on?"

"What business you have calling the man at ten o'clock last night?" The words release like seeds from a pod.

"Me? What does Wool disappearing have to do with me?"

"Oh God, those awful vipers."

She's never liked them. She was there when the mapepire zananas arrived two years ago. The hunter called the zoo to say he was on his way with two bad snakes. Miss Zanana and Boyfriend arrived tied in the tray of a 1970's pickup. Back then we already had a big dog-head anaconda, some mapepire balsains, a few stringy corals, boas, and tigres, but we'd been looking for a mapepire zanana, the true bushmaster. Mr. Wool, Rhonda, and I went to meet the rattling truck in the car park. Zananas were rare; they almost never bred under watching eyes. The hunter had driven the three hours from the mountain village of Brasso Secco with all the windows sealed tight even though the snakes were double wrapped in the tray and bound in jute. When I looked over the side of the pickup, the jute sacks moved as if they held men.

"Most dangerous snake in the world, one bite and… WHADAP!" The hunter hit his hand on the side of rumbling open tray for effect. "One strike and is only a matter of time before you dead. Watch where a balsain get me years ago," he'd said, pulling denim out of battered boots. "And they say zanana plenty worse. Pretty like woman, but once them fangs hit, corbeaux get the zeppo to come."

He'd turned on his heel, swinging his calf, puckered and ruined, into view. In the silence, the hunter spat on the dusty ground between us.

"But still, I don't like to kill them. Far less the zanana, you know?" Here the man pulled at his hair and wiped his forehead. "How you could kill something so beautiful?"

We'd all nodded silently, looking at the ugly scar.

"How much?" Mr. Wool had asked.

Rhonda locks me out the office. She beats me to the door by seconds, sliding the wrought iron security gate into place and turning the key as I arrive. Her knuckles turn cream where she squeezes the iron bars and leans in to hiss at me.

"Always with them blasted snakes. Touch the snake, play with the snake. What did you do with him?"

Rhonda moves her hands from the door to pat an imaginary snake around her neck, embarrassing me with her bizarre pantomime. Watching her soft hands stroke the air close to her neck, I want to slap her.

"What the fuck the snakes have to do with Wool?"

Through the door, I can see across the room. Wool's office is laid out neatly: papers stacked waiting his signature, young Wool smiling at me from the photo on the wall, the strange green light from the cannon ball tree spilling out onto the floor.

"Breathe, breathe," says the voice in my head.

I look up into the canopy of the cannon ball tree in front of the office. It had been planted as a tiny sapling. Now it is very large with wonderfully strange perfumed flowers that emerge from its bark. I imagine the life above. There are probably more than a few snakes in the tree. I've always hoped so. Every day I enter this office, I look up in search of life. A snake, a lizard, a corn bird pirouetting in a love dance. It is good to be reminded that not all animals are dependent on our care for survival.

On the other side of the door, Rhonda moves to the window, her hand to her mouth. Soon she moves again and I follow around the building, moving quietly from window to window so I can see what she will do. She is shredding papers. She doesn't know I can see her through the window, almost hidden in the gloom. In front of the open butterfly cabinet, her hands are working quickly.

"Rhonda," my voice is soft. "I'm going to check on the snakes. Can you call and cancel the school tour please?"

When she turns to look at me over her shoulder, her face judders slightly.

In the cool, dim light, I greet Miss Zanana. I can never tell if she is happy to see me. The snake's eyes are flat and opaque. I sit for a long time in front of the glass enclosure. I've always kept the venomous snakes separated from the others. I've been so careful, I've tried so hard to keep the balance between humans and the snakes, never taking chances. Though they are furnished with rotting wood, damp moss, and maidenhair ferns, all my snakes languish in well-secured glass houses.

Someone is behind me in the cool dark room; she is ducking under the vine. She walks to the front of the glass enclosure and reads the metal label on the front of the cage.

"Mapepire Zanana, Bushmaster. *Lachesis muta muta*. God, how can you stand them?"

"They're snakes. They're not evil."

"Where is he, Brian?" She is unclipping the master keys from her belt and handing them to me. "I found these in here this morning. What did you do with him?"

I am looking for the snake hook, unhooking the leather case that holds the sharp cutlass that I keep close to the vipers, in case of emergencies. After this I don't speak because I am pulling Miss Zanana out of her cage with the snake hook, the sharp edge pinning her flat adder head and causing her cold-blood heart to beat quickly. My father always taught me: Bury the dead with the head and tail of the killer. If not, the mate will seek you all the days of its life.

SPELUNKING

The man behind the end door is old and life-worn, rheumy-eyed. He looks like a drinker. When he bows, his sharp spine ladders into his merino. Noemi hangs back behind the others. They hand over the rum and cigars like contraband while the fat wife smiles and smiles. They follow the trails of flesh that quiver in the wife's wake and soon there are five of them crowded in the small room with a foam double bed and a hot plate. The wife sweeps the clothes piled in the centre of the bed into a suitcase, which she has pulled from under the bed.

The santero lives in the slums behind South Beach. To get to him, they have passed all the ritzy, jangly people and the fancy restaurants. These Jose points out to Noemi because she is a visitor. As they drive, Jose tells Noemi that he wants to become a santero. The man they are visiting is his padrino, his Santeria sponsor. Jose will soon be marrying her friend Mariquite, and Noemi thinks of Mariquite's parents in Trinidad and wonders how her friend will navigate these two worlds. Jose works for a shipping company in Doral and Mariquite still flies for Caribbean Airlines. They live together in a neat townhouse in South Kendall. This was where Noemi had expected to meet the santero.

His room is on the third floor of a high-rise shot up with graffiti. The elevator does not work so they had to take the stairs. As they walked down the corridor, Jose called out to people whose open doors spilled cloudy air, heavy with marijuana and garlic. A woman was sitting on a plastic chair outside a door breastfeeding a baby, while three children kicked a ball around her chair.

"We've only just got him out of Cuba," says Jose. "Soon we will get him settled. We will find something nicer for him."

Mariquite turns around in her seat and squeezes Noemi's hand.

"He's good. You'll see."

Noemi has brought along a rosary, not because she is especially religious but because she is wary of the unknown.

"As long as he doesn't want me to kill a white chicken," says Noemi, half joking.

"Hmmmm. Maybe a brown one?" Mariquite smiles and Noemi can't tell if she is being serious.

As they wait in the room, Noemi thinks of her husband eating dinner in the fancy hotel restaurant. She imagines the food: shrimp cocktail and a medium rare rib-eye with a glass of merlot. She'd agreed to come on a lark with Mariquite. It seemed exotic. Exciting. Something different to do. But now she has a swooping sensation of panic, her breath rising quickly in her chest. She has not anticipated this feeling.

By now, a small area in the corner of the room has been transformed with blue, red, and white satin cloths.

"It's an altar," whispers Mariquite. "An igbodu."

Noemi genuflects as she does before the altar in her parish church in Trinidad. The santero is happy to have Noemi and makes signs of welcome.

"They don't speak English," says Mariquite. "Jose will translate."

"Sit. Sit. We must begin," says Jose, while Mariquite and the wife light the candles around the room. Soon the air in the room is dense with incense, the candlelight cutting trails of light through the smoke. The santero breaks the seal on the bottle of proof rum they bought at the liquor store on the way, puts it to his lips and drinks as if it is noon and the rum is cold water.

Noemi watches his Adam's apple move up and down as he drinks. Five minutes later he is still chatting quietly in Spanish with Jose. She is uncomfortable on the edge of the double bed, negotiating with her fear as she leans into the fat of the santero's wife. She wants to pee but is embarrassed that they will hear the sound of her stream through the cheap laminate door. She is thinking this when the man's demeanour changes.

When it happens, it is not what she expected. She'd anticipated tricks. She is looking at him when something slaps the back of his head. Even though the room is soft with candlelight, it is bright enough for Noemi to see the man clearly. He lurches forward, his chin hitting his chest with a snap that makes her worry for his neck. When he straightens, a new man with intelligent eyes addresses them in Yoruba before switching to melodious English. He speaks to Noemi of blind catfish.

★

From my verandah I like to imagine that I am lying on the flat surface of the sea and the undulating land below me buckles up from the ocean floor. I do this until I feel ill and the child inside me kicks in protest. I've been here for one year and the view never grows tired.

It is a good position I have with the university. For my twenty-first birthday, my mother gave me a leather bag with a brass tag embossed with my name: Noemi de Lourge. I use this bag to store my papers and journals. My mother is very proud that I am working on my PhD and I am only twenty-three. My thesis is concerned with life in the freshwater rivers of the northern range. My days are occupied with the minute details of the lives of guppies and guabines – and the child tadpoling inside me. Every morning I walk to the riverhead that is the source of the Paria Falls to visit my field station. There I spend the morning making notes on the purity of water and the health of the varieties of river life that swim through the clear pools. Occasionally I see a guppy sport with a long tail that makes him stand out from the other more common ones. But this is not very often.

The drive to Morne Bleu takes two hours from Port of Spain. It is beautiful country with dense, overhanging forest trees and an understory of oversized ferns. This type of forest is referred to as moist. It never dries and the trees drip rain long after the sky has stopped. When you walk the paths, the ground can sink and hold your ankles.

An old man at the village centre tells me he was just a child in 1934 when Mikey Cipriani's plane crashed into the mountains. I take this as a warning. No town shenanigans like flashy planes or making the village my own exotic backdrop. The forest has an instinct for this type of behaviour – Mikey Cipriani, a dashing Port of Spain bachelor, flying over the hidden rivers and caves – all that good luck provoking an irritable magnet of bad weather, which plucked the plane out the sky. The old man tells me that the men from the village hunted until they found the wreckage and brought the remains of Cipriani and his companion out.

The people here are simple, hardworking farmers, but there are few opportunities for the young men. They loiter on the outskirts and hiss at me when I walk by. The old man tells me about Cipriani because there is a manhunt on now for a boy. He's been disappeared. That's the word the village uses. As if he were an item on a shelf to be picked up and thrown into a bag. The police swarm through the small village each morning and comb the hills. The police inspector advises me to go back to Port of Spain. Do they know that the boy they are looking for is well known to me?

They are superstitious about me in this village. My looks don't match my accent. Here in the northeastern tip of the island, I am an anomaly. Who leaves the city to come and live in a village? And a white woman at that. I might be excused if I was a foreigner, but local whites are expected to know better.

"So where are you from?" This is the village's collective question; they've asked it so many times.

"I'm from right here. Island born and bred."

"Hmmm," they say, glancing at me out of the whites of their eyes like frightened horses. "Where is your family? What are you doing here?"

"I work with the university."

"Where is your family from?"

"Port of Spain."

"Yes, but where are you really from?"

"From here. Just like you."

When the university sends foreign students to visit my station, the villagers are chatty and engaging with the Germans and the British. It is only with me that they are reserved, cautious. This changes only with my pregnancy. When it is clear that I will stay and give birth in the village, the women mother me like one of their own. I tell them that the father is an old boyfriend and we have broken up. The old women cluck and fuss but the younger ones squeeze my hand.

I know the day I got pregnant. I'd been thinking of blind catfish.

160

The boy who is missing is called Daniel. He is only seventeen and I am a full woman of twenty-three. A grown woman with all my bones fused into adulthood. In those early days of my research, Daniel was the guide assigned to me by the university.

"Where do you want to go?" he says on our first meeting.

"I want to go to the caves. First to Cumaca to see the blind catfish. And then to Tamana to see the bats."

The road to the Cumaca Cave in the northern range is very overgrown now, dusty and pitted. Whole chunks of the mountain have been dug out for aggregate and the beautiful blue stone that we use to face buildings. The run-off from these quarries pollutes the rivers, but only below where it enters. If you follow rivers like the Turure upstream, the peace lilies appear on the sides of the water and the water becomes clear again.

The first time we visit Cumaca cave, I'm reluctant to enter. The mouth is hooded with heavy greenery, the interior dark and hidden, curling in on itself. From outside the cave, we can hear the cries of the oilbirds. The cave houses thousands of these beautiful, clumsy birds and their fat babies. Inside, the cave opens into chambers, wide-open spaces with stalagmites and stalactites straining to touch each other, surrounded by squalling birds.

To enter, we'd walked under the small plaque, green with moss. I'd come here to see this as well. In the early 1960s, two young divers slipped under a crevice in the last chamber searching for the source of the water. The cave swallowed them whole; the bubbles from their air tanks dislodging tiny stones and bringing down an avalanche. Daniel tells me his father spoke to the diver who'd come from San Fernando to try and retrieve the bodies.

"He could only get one out. The other was too tangled in

the rocks." He says this to me as we stand in the shallow pool, the blind catfish willowing around our legs. "He's still in there."

The cave breathes silently in the darkness, the birds shrieking above us.

It's a strange thing. The cave is well known for its population of blind catfish, regular river catfish except they are blind and colourless, glimmers of silver under the torch. In the 1920s and 30s, almost all the Cumaca catfish were blind. Now it is said that there are not so many. Too many visitors to the caves have changed the ecosystem and now they are growing eyes. I'm studying this phenomenon, catching what I can and recording weights. Shining a light into tiny faces.

I know the day I got pregnant. I'd been thinking about blind catfish. Carefully recording all the details of the cave, listing the physical things I was able to observe. Hundreds of oilbirds circling in the dark, the heavy presence of the long dead boys – these were not things that I could record but they were the things that occupied my mind, like the brushes of silver against my bare legs.

I am a woman who is careful of her appearance. I do things like polish my toenails and brush my hair one hundred times every night. My mother is proud of my hair. It is very blonde and thick and during the day I wear it in a thick braid. I've only had two boyfriends, both of them sons of my mother's friends, boys I've known all my life.

On that first visit, a man meets us on the way back from the caves. He slips out of the forest like a mirage, silent and sullen.

"Wait," says Daniel. "Wait here. I'll be back."

Like a face forming in the pattern of a curtain, the house takes shape in the distant foliage. Daniel goes into the house with the man and when he comes back, he has a brown knapsack and a tightly wrapped package. I go with him three times after this. I need more data on the catfish. Each time the man meets Daniel and I wait by the side of the track, making careful notes in my journal. I am not afraid because it seems to me that the forest reserves its irritability for the fey and merry. I feel completely safe with the copper boy who wears a wild hog's tooth around his neck on a string of leather. He had beautiful long fingers and a light brown birthmark on his left cheek, a velvet-furred spot that shines like deerskin under candlelight.

Once a month, I drive down the mountain road and make my way out of Arima towards Valencia, where I begin my climb to the Turure River. My job here also is to check on the freshwater life – the crayfish, and manicou crabs, the guabines, the guppies. Higher up the Turure falls, limestone turns the water jade green. The limestone originates in Platana, and the river comes down in large river steps. The green limestone gives these steps the appearance of being mossy, but it is possible to walk mostly upright without slipping or falling back, tricking both the eye and the heart. Occasionally a pocket of iron bubbles behind a stone, the rust-coloured water coming up like blood. Near the falls, the water is clear and you often hear the bellbird signalling its mate, the deep-gong call vibrating through the forest. But at the bridge where I have set up my station, the silt and debris from the quarrying has turned the water soupy. Water life here is scarce but when I do find it, I note the impact of the quarrying, changes to eyes, body-weight, fertility.

It is after visiting the Turure station that I go to the doctor. There is no ultrasound machine in Morne Bleu. The doctor in Arima makes notes as detailed as my own, carefully recording growth. Today, his hands are cold on my stomach which, now I am almost at full-term, hovers above my chest like a golden moon. The hard roll of compressed, pregnancy panty-elastic presses into my pubic bone. Here and there through the static on the screen, a limb comes into focus and flails wildly. This will be my last visit. After this I will visit the village midwife. When I fill out the form for the doctor, I write an imaginary name on the line that says "Father".

"What did the doctor say?" My brother, Henri, calls me every other day.

"Everything is fine. Thirty-nine weeks today."

"Hold on," he says. "Hold on. Marcella wants to speak to you."

"Hello, Noemi," says my sister-in-law. "Noemi, Noemi you have to come to us. You can't stay there. What are you going to do afterwards?" When I hear her husky voice, I can picture her sitting in their kitchen on the estate. My mother does not approve of my brother's cocoa estate and she does not approve of Marcella with her milky-brown skin and her wild curly hair. My mother does not know that I am pregnant. Marcella and Henri have kept my secret.

When Daniel's mother comes to see me, he's been missing for three days. She knocks on my door and asks if I have seen her son. She has been crying and her features bunch in the centre of her face when she tells me he cannot be found. Do I know anything? I think of Mikey Cipriani flying his plane confidently into the storm. I think of the two divers slipping into the hidden cavern. I listen to the forest breathe outside the window while I remember the house in the foliage. No, I say. No, I don't know anything.

"How are you feeling?" she asks as she reaches to touch my stomach. "You must be nearly due."

"Anytime now."

"And the father will soon come?"

"He will try but it's difficult to get up from Port of Spain."

I wonder how much she knows as I lie smoothly.

The cashew tree behind the house is bowed with the bumper crop. I am sick of the smell of rotten cashew fruit. At night, the baby tangles in my ribs.

On the morning of the first twinge, I pack my bag and call Henri.

"I'm going to the clinic. The midwife will check me."

"Noemi, are you sure? We can come for you."

"No, it will be fine."

The clinic is not far and I meet others going to see the midwife. Outside Daniel's house, a crowd gathers on the stairs while the police dogs bark down from the surrounding forest. I think of Daniel and his velvet spot and I remember the man in the forest. The road is hot and dusty and the baby is kicking and squirming, throwing irritable jabs with each step

"Hey girl," says the small one who lives next to the market. She walks next to me, twisting her hair into a thick rope braid that she pulls away from her sweating neck. She carries her pregnancy high on her ribcage and walks with the rolling gait of a woman loving her new body. "You're nearly ready now." It is not a question.

The women touch my stomach as I walk through the net of hands reaching for me, gently patting me as I walk by.

"You've dropped. Didn't you feel it?"

In the clinic, the little one sits next to me, twisting her rope-braid hair in a way that tells me she is worried. The woman across the room is also thirty-nine weeks pregnant, but she is pregnant with twins. She leans back on the slatted bench panting and heaving behind the enormous stomach that has deformed her body. If I slit my eyes I imagine I can see two little old men sitting back-to-back in her belly.

The women talk of the language of dreams. I do not tell anyone about my dreams. They come to me in multi-colour – vibrant pinks and greens and hot orange. There is a new girl today. She cannot be older than sixteen. She sits across the room and listens quietly. Unlike the rest of us, she is not pregnant but rather soft and swollen, as if something has pulled and tugged her out of shape. She begins relating her dream in a light, sweet voice, speaking to no one in particular.

"I dreamed I saw my baby last night…"

There is something in the sound of her voice that is not right.

"She looked good. She looked so good. So good. I said, Tiffany? Tiffany, that is you? That is really you? And she wanted to run and skip and play… and… and I didn't have the heart to tell her… but Tiffany, you dead."

She stops and closes her eyes. The room is silent. Those with children draw them to their laps, the rest hug their swollen bellies. The airless room narrows as the girl looks straight across the room at me. We sit breathing in and out while the baby swims lazily in my centre.

The women on either side of me make the sign of the cross, and one throws a small cloth over my belly as if to shield me from the girl's gaze. Outside the sun shines down mercilessly, killing all the tender shadows that hide in the ferns underneath the red flamboyant tree outside. The baby is quiet in me, lulled by the girl's strange voice.

My pains start late in the afternoon. I rock slowly and look at the forest until the light is gone and I can no longer see between the shadows. It is only then that I call my neighbour to go for the midwife. By the time the midwife arrives, I am hot pink and bright orange, purple and red, seared with streaks of yellow. The midwife raises my head and puts a cup of thyme tea to my lips. Then she gives me castor oil. The pain is an alien thing, alive and intelligent. There is a plane flying into my centre. It is blocking the divers from swimming out. It cannot be a baby. No baby was ever this big; no baby this big could ever have been born.

The midwife squats in front of me. "I can see the head," she says. "Push. Push."

A flash of colour builds and throbs into a white-hot point as my daughter slips into the world.

"Hello, little Tiffany," says the midwife. "What a mass of dark hair – just like your mother."

For a second I think I have misheard her words.

"Can I see her?"

"Let me clean her up and I'll come back to you."

"No, please. I'd like to hold her first."

The midwife stands holding Tiffany, already swaddled, only the soft down of her crown visible to me.

"So sad about that girl in the clinic who lost her baby," the midwife says. "She's really taking it on. Calling the child back to her."

"Can I see my baby, please?" The midwife is frightening me.

"So sad. And the father disappearing just like that."

"Who was the father?"

"The young boy who is missing. The girl is from higher up in the mountain. They say the spirit of the boy took the baby with him."

"What does that have to do with my baby?" I am crying now. "Give her. Give her to me."

It is hard to pull myself off the bed because I am still bleeding heavily. She allows me to put my daughter to my breast while she delivers my placenta.

"It is as it should be," she says.

"Does everyone know?"

"Yes, it is the only thing to do. The baby was born here. She is from here. She should stay here."

At twenty-three, I thought I was a fully-formed woman with my bones fused into adulthood. But just like that, I let someone take my baby away. After, she helps me bind my breasts and I help her dress the baby. My daughter. Before the night is up, the girl knocks on my door and the midwife hands her the tiny bundle.

I call Henri to come and get me. The forest has no time for town shenanigans like flashy planes or making the village my own exotic backdrop. The forest has an instinct for this type of behaviour, even if you hide it from yourself. When Henri comes, I pack my journals of data, five binders filled with detailed notes on the catfish and leave quietly with him. Later, he and Marcella will come up to collect the rest of my things.

A decade after I will publish a paper on the social and environmental impact of increased foot traffic to Cumaca Caves. I will posit that over time the *Caecorhamdia urichi,* the freshwater catfish, adapted to life in the caves, losing both pigment and their eyes. It is now accepted that these freshwater fish can regrow eyes and regain pigment when they are exposed to light. But then, they are nothing more than regular river catfish.

★

"You worry about the blind catfish?" says the rich, dark voice coming from the tiny Cuban santero.

"No, not that." Noemi's voice is low and gravelly in the dark, her blonde hair shining towards the santero.

"The girl has perfect sight but she only sees what she has been conditioned to see. You will never be visible to her."

"The boy," says Noemi. "The boy. What happened to the boy?"

"He is merry and fey."

★

Once a year, the midwife sends a photograph of Tiffany to me. It comes to my university address and I hide these photographs in a safety deposit box at the bank. Long after I'd married and had my own children, I search the features of the girl in the photographs, looking for some sign of myself. But there is nothing. She is small and pretty, copper-coloured and dark-haired with a small dark pelted birthmark on her cheek.

Sharon Millar is a graduate of the Lesley University MFA program and is a past student of the late Wayne Brown. She is the winner of the 2013 Commonwealth Short Story Prize and the 2012 Small Axe Short Fiction Award. In 2013 she was also shortlisted for the Hollick Arvon Caribbean Writer's Prize for fiction.

A past NGC Bocas Lit New Talent Showcase writer, her work has appeared in publications such as *Granta*, *The Manchester Review*, *Small Axe*, and *Susumba Book Bag*. Her story "The Whale House" was anthologized in *Pepperpot: Best New Stories from The Caribbean*.

She is a part time lecturer at The University of the West Indies, St Augustine, where she teaches Prose Fiction.

"Sharon Millar has written a collection where 'hard back woman give talk' and 'big man stand up and cry.' After reading it you may do the same. Millar has rooted herself into a Caribbean literature where language crackles and no ethnicity, gender, economic status or race is off limits. The collection is one of handsome boys with bullets in their backs and of high-class women with babies in their bellies. There is a sweet and bitter magic here that Millar performs via the bodies of the characters. Women have turmeric eyes, men are too beautiful to die, children dance the cocoa and unborn babies are born as baby sharks. This book made me catch my breath. It made me shake my head and sigh. The characters barb and the language sings."

— Tiphanie Yanique, author of *Land of Love and Drowning*